Petal Plucker was funny, entertaining, fresh and fan-yourself-worthy . . . Their enemies-to-lovers romance is both charming, tender and steamy, and you'll love both of these characters (and their families!) and their sigh-worthy happily ever after.

— MARY DUBÉ, CONTEMPORARILY EVER AFTER

Morland has created a masterpiece of a romance . . . one of my favorite [books] of the year.

— CRISTIINA READS

Humorous, raunchy, and refreshing, Petal Plucker has rightfully earned its way, in my opinion, as one of the best romantic comedy [books] this year.

— CAROL, TIL THE LAST PAGE

My One and Only

This book was gripping, well written & the chemistry between the characters sizzled throughout this wonderful read.

— AMAZON REVIEW

PRAISE FOR IRIS MORLAND

Forever Mine

Warn your people not to disturb you then settle in and start reading this phenomenal, heartfelt, swoony romance today! Your romantic heart will thank you.

— BOOKADDICT

The Prince I Love to Hate

The Prince I Love To Hate is an absolute must read! This romcom will have you rooting for Niamh and Olivier right from their hilarious first meeting.

— HARLEQUIN BOOK JUNKIE BLOG

Oopsie Daisy

Quirky, fun, witty, hilarious! Iris Morland always manages to get me to laugh out loud.

—WHISPERING CHAPTERS

He Loves Me, He Loves Me Not

A hilarious, sexy and heartwarming romantic comedy...you do not want to miss this fun, feel-good romance.

— MARY DUBÉ, CONTEMPORARILY EVER AFTER

...refreshing, funny, emotionally charged, and very entertaining to read.

— CAROL, TIL THE LAST PAGE

There is humor, there is heart and there is heat in this story! I absolutely loved it! . . . Mari and Liam delivered. Yowza, their chemistry was palpable.

— BIBLIOPHILE CHLOE

PETAL PLUCKER

Funny, charming, and utterly captivating! I devoured this sparkling read.

—ANNIKA MARTIN, NEW YORK TIMES BESTSELLING AUTHOR

Till There Was You

I'll Be Home for Christmas

~

THE HEIR AFFAIR DUET

The Prince I Love to Hate

The Princess I Hate to Love

~

HERON'S LANDING

Say You're Mine

All I Ask of You

Make Me Yours

Hold Me Close

~

THE FLOWER SHOP SISTERS

War of the Roses

Petal Plucker

He Loves Me, He Loves Me Not

Oopsie Daisy

LOVE IS HERE TO STAY

HAZEL ISLAND

IRIS MORLAND

BLUE VIOLET PRESS LLC

For my mom, who never fails to ask how the book-writing is going.

LOVE IS HERE TO STAY

CHAPTER ONE

Alexandra Gray was the type of person who preferred not to think about unpleasant things. It was going to rain? She'd worry about that tomorrow. Her favorite boots were close to falling apart? She'd take care of that when the literal soles fell off of them.

She knew, however, that her Scarlett O'Hara philosophy of "I'll think about that tomorrow" wasn't the best way to approach running a business. Especially when said business kept losing money month after month. Every quarter, profit dwindled while expenses increased.

Alex stared at her computer screen, hoping that the spreadsheet was adding things incorrectly. That number couldn't be right. But as she reentered the numbers and tabulated them a second, third, even fourth time, the number didn't change.

"Shit," she mumbled in despair. She pressed her forehead to her desk and suddenly wished she were far, far away from her beloved bookstore.

When she'd purchased the Hazel Island Bookstore from its previous owner years ago, it had been something of an impulse. Alex had needed a new thing to focus on. She'd been drifting, no goal in mind. Then Max had told her he'd planned on closing the place when he retired. Alex, overly optimistic as she was wont to be, told him she'd buy it from him.

Her older sister Jocelyn had told Alex that she had been an idiot. And Jocelyn would say the same thing right now if she saw this spreadsheet.

"Alex?" A knock sounded on Alex's office door. "I need another set of hands out here. Afternoon rush," said Chris, her only employee.

Alex snorted. There was no such thing as a rush in this bookstore. It was more of a slow, meandering trickle. Occasionally they got extra foot traffic from large groups of tourists. Their best months were the height of the summer season and then another bump around the holidays. During the summer, though, was when people forgot their e-readers at home and needed something to read on the beach in a pinch.

"I'll be out in a second," Alex called to Chris.

"Five minutes or I'm stealing from the till," Chris joked.

"Nothing to steal from the till," she said to herself, sighing. She needed to figure out a strategy to get out of this hole she'd dug. She'd thought of a handful of ideas, but they all needed one thing: money. And Alex was light on the money front.

When she went back out into the store, inhaling the scents of pine, ink, and paper, her mood lifted. No matter how much of a burden it was, she loved this bookstore. She loved the huge windows that beckoned customers to come inside. The excitement on people's faces when the book they'd been dying to read was finally released. Alex loved unboxing new shipments of books, flipping through the pages, and sometimes getting distracted from sorting and shelving more times than she could count.

Chris was shelving in the back. Three customers were browsing, two of whom were regular customers.

"You made it sound like this place was packed," said Alex.

Chris, a tall, skinny guy with hair longer than Alex's, shrugged. "I thought you could use a break from number-crunching." He took in her expression. "Considering the look on your face, I'm gonna assume it didn't go well."

Alex forced herself to smile. "Nothing you need to worry about."

"I'm on your payroll, darling. If anyone should worry, it's me."

"The help shouldn't ask questions. Get back to work," joked Alex.

Chris saluted her with an eye roll. Despite his sarcasm, Chris was a dedicated, efficient employee. He'd recently graduated from college and had come back to live with his parents, not sure what he wanted to do with his life. Although he was only four years younger than Alex, she felt motherly toward him. He still had some of the dewy-eyed hopefulness of one's early twenties.

She knew from experience that that hopefulness tended to fade with age.

I'm not even thirty and already I'm so cynical, she thought wryly.

After one customer checked out, Alex was organizing books in the back when the entrance bell chimed. "Welcome," she heard Chris say. "Let me know if you need help finding anything."

"Will do," said a masculine voice.

Alex froze. Peering through the shelves, she watched the man, wishing he'd turn toward her.

She knew that voice. She'd heard it in her dreams for the past three months.

Finally, she saw his face. She inhaled. It was him. She knew it like she knew her own name.

Under the stars, the waves gently lapping at the shore, this man had kissed her like a man starved. It had been a kiss she could never, ever forget.

She watched the man begin to browse. Did she continue working and have him find her? Or did she take the bull by the horns and surprise him?

Alex smiled devilishly. Coming around the shelf, she approached the handsome stranger, her heart beating like crazy in anticipation.

"Do you need help finding anything?" she asked, sounding rather breathless.

"No, I'm…"

She saw the moment recognition hit him when he finally looked at her. Then he stared at her, like he wasn't sure she was actually a real person.

"You," said the man, incredulous.

Redness crept up Alex's face. Why was she blushing? Kissing a handsome stranger was hardly out of character for her. But seeing the mystery man in person was like a slap in the face.

By moonlight, he'd been handsome. By daylight, he was breathtaking.

Light blue eyes, a jawline that could cut glass. His hair was a light brown, with a slight curl to it. Alex wondered how curly it became when it grew out. She also wondered how silky it would feel under her fingertips.

"Me," she said with a smile.

The man finally tore his gaze from her. "Are you following me?" was his next question.

"Following you?" She let out an incredulous laugh. "You're the one who came in here."

He shook himself, a smile slowly forming on his face. The transformation from frowning annoyance to amused interest was like a lightning bolt to Alex's stomach.

"You never did tell me your name," said Alex.

"Neither did you."

"I asked first."

He chuckled. "What would the fun in that be? Names are boring. Besides, what if you have a terrible name?"

Alex shot him an outraged look. "I don't have a terrible name!"

"Of course you'd say that. And then next you're telling me your name is Drusilla or Agnes, and I have to act like I'm still interested when in fact I'd like to run in the opposite direction."

"Why do I have the feeling *you're* the one with a terrible name? From now on, I'm going to call you something ridiculous." Alex tapped her chin. "Barnaby? Milton? No, how about Nebuchadnezzar? I'll call you Nezzie for short."

As Alex spoke, she began to reorganize a shelf that had

books out of alphabetical order. Her shirt rose as she stood on tiptoe, showing off a flash of midriff.

Her mystery man's laughter at her joke faded away. Alex had to restrain a grin when she could feel his heated gaze on the bit of bared flesh.

Checkmate, she thought.

But before she could say something else, the man's phone rang, insistent and loud inside the quiet of the bookstore. He took the call and stepped away from Alex. Based on the expression on his face, it wasn't good news. The frown from earlier was back on his face.

"I have to go," he said to Alex quickly. He stuffed his phone back into his pocket, and then, without another word, he stalked from the store.

Alex stared at the door for a long moment, completely nonplussed. She didn't even hear Chris sidle up next to her.

"Soooooooooo," he said, "what was all that about?"

"We were just talking."

Chris shot her an incredulous look. "You guys looked like you were about to rip each other's clothes off right here in the DIY aisle."

"Chris! Keep your voice down."

"There's nobody in here now."

She was annoyed to see that Chris was right. She hadn't been paying any attention to her other customers. She'd been so enthralled with this mystery man that it had been as if they'd been the only two people in existence.

"Who was that guy, anyway?" said Chris into the silence. "I've never seen him before. Tourist? It's kind of late in the year for tourists."

"I have no idea." Which was true. Alex wasn't sure if

he'd moved here permanently or was simply staying here for months at a time. Or he just really liked visiting.

Luckily for Alex, a few more customers entered, giving her a respite from Chris's questions. Alex didn't know how to answer them. She hadn't told anyone, not even her two best friends, about the kiss with the stranger on the beach. It had been such a lovely, dreamlike moment that she felt like talking about it would take away its magic.

After the store closed for the night and Chris had left, Alex was once again in her office, her mind no longer on mystery men or their kisses. Instead, she was researching ways to expand the bookstore in some direction that would be profitable.

She'd considered adding a coffee stand, but there were three other cafes on the island already on the same street. As far as hosting famous authors, it was a tough sell considering that Hazel Island was tiny and remote. You could only get there by ferry. When authors had the choice of signing in Seattle or on Hazel Island, they chose the big city every time.

The exception had been the famous—and famously reclusive—romance author Lila White. But she'd canceled her signing only a week before, and she hadn't replied to any of Alex's attempts to rebook her.

Alex was about to go home when she checked her inbox one last time. Opening the email, she felt the breath leave her body in one fell swoop.

New rental management

Building has been purchased

Rent increase

And at the bottom, it was signed by some real estate

developer from Seattle who'd probably never even seen this building in person. And he wanted to increase Alex's rent by twenty-five percent.

Alex felt sick. She was just barely paying her rent currently. A twenty-five-percent increase? That was insane. It couldn't be legal, she thought frantically.

Worse, her lease was up for renewal in three months. Which meant she either had to figure out a way to pay for the rent increase, or she had to shut her doors.

"No, no, no, no," she kept repeating. She wanted to tear her hair out.

Correction: she wanted to tear out the hair of this guy who'd sent her this email.

It was such a cold, perfunctory email. No apologies, no explanations given. He expected she'd hand over the cash without protest.

She scowled at the signature: Aaron Morrison. "Fuck you, Aaron Morrison," she hissed as she began to type out her reply. "Fuck you with a rusty spoon, you greedy asshole."

Although she was tempted to include those exact words in her email, she had just enough self-control not to. Her email, though, was a master class in passive-aggressive business talk.

An increase this large is outrageous, she wrote. *I will be inquiring with the appropriate authorities to ascertain if an amount so outrageous is even legal.*

She sent the email after making sure she hadn't included any typos. She probably shouldn't have threatened her new landlord, but she was too angry to care. She wasn't about to roll over and let this Aaron walk all over her.

When she received a reply not even five minutes later, she let out a grim laugh.

Let's discuss this over the phone at your convenience, was all that it said.

"I'm going to make you wish you'd never been born," she vowed.

CHAPTER TWO

The principal of Hazel Island Middle School wasn't an imposing man, but Mr. Foster had perfected the disappointed frown. And he was using it quite effectively on Aaron Morrison. Although Aaron hadn't been in grade school student in nearly twenty years, he still had to refrain from squirming in his seat.

His eleven-year-old nephew Logan wasn't fazed. He just kept swinging his feet and staring out the window, where other students were currently playing dodgeball.

Mr. Foster folded his hands. "There has been another incident," he intoned heavily. He looked toward Logan, and his expression seemed resigned. "In the cafeteria this time."

Considering there had already been three other incidents in the past two months, Aaron was grudgingly impressed with his nephew's ability to get into trouble no matter the location.

"Logan," said Mr. Foster sharply. "You need to pay attention."

Logan seemed tempted to roll his eyes, but when Aaron shook his head slightly, his nephew apparently decided not to push things.

Mr. Foster then proceeded to describe how Logan had come up behind another student and had dumped an entire bowl of applesauce on his head.

Logan snickered. Aaron wanted to melt into the floor. Or shake his nephew until his teeth rattled.

"Is something funny, young man?" asked Mr. Foster.

Logan folded his arms, a smirk on his face. Aaron hated that stupid smirk. In the last year, Logan had gotten way too good at making a face that screamed he didn't care what you said to him. The kind of face only an eleven-year-old with an attitude could come up with.

"Noooooo," was Logan's reply, but the smile wouldn't leave his lips.

"This is very serious. This is the fourth incident this year. You've already been suspended twice." Although Mr. Foster didn't raise his voice, his tone hardened with each word. "You could be expelled. Do you know what that means?"

Logan grinned. "I don't have to go to school anymore?"

"Logan!" hissed Aaron. Now he wasn't just embarrassed —he was pissed. "Mr. Foster, I'll deal with him. He'll apologize to the student, too."

"What? No, I won't!" squawked Logan.

Aaron decided to ignore that outburst. After more promises to Mr. Foster and assurances he'd get Logan in check, he and Logan headed home.

As a real estate developer, Aaron could work remotely. When he'd had to take in his niece and nephew after their parents' sudden deaths, being able to work from home had seemed like one of the few bright spots in Aaron's life.

Now, though, Aaron suddenly wished he had an office to get away from it all.

I'm out of my fucking depth, he kept thinking to himself on the silent ride home. Logan just stared out the window the entire time.

"Well?" Aaron said finally, gripping the steering wheel hard. "Do you have anything to say for yourself?"

Logan shrugged. "Nope."

Aaron gritted his teeth. He forced himself to stay calm. He knew that Logan wanted a reaction from him, and he was not about to be bested by an eleven-year-old.

"You realize you could be kicked out of school? The only middle school on the island?" said Aaron.

"School is stupid."

"Everybody your age thinks school is stupid. But you still have to go. I'm not homeschooling you. If you get expelled, you're going to boarding school."

Aaron knew it was an empty threat, but Logan didn't know that.

Logan shot him an outraged look. "That's not fair!"

"What's not fair is you dumping applesauce on someone. Why? Why did you think that was okay?"

Logan's expression turned mulish. "You wouldn't understand."

Their conversation continued after they'd arrived home, although it was mostly Aaron following Logan to his room, admonishing him with every step. Logan, for his part, was just getting angrier.

"You're not my dad!" shouted Logan once he'd reached his room. "So just shut up already!"

Logan slammed his bedroom door in Aaron's face. When Aaron heard the click of the lock, he knew his nephew had won this round.

Lately, it seemed like his nephew *always* won. Aaron was just thankful that his niece, Penelope, was perfectly behaved. Even at thirteen, she was mature beyond her years.

"Jason, why did you have to die?" Aaron whispered to himself as he went to his office and shut the door. On his desk was a framed photo of his brother's family taken only a few months before Jason and his wife, Ashley, had died.

Jason had always been the one who'd known what to do. But he wasn't here. So Aaron was muddling through, all the while knowing he was making a mess of things.

Aaron picked up the photo but seeing his brother's smiling face made him angry. Angry, because it wasn't fair that Jason had died so young. Angry, because if anyone should've died, it should've been Aaron.

Aaron sighed. He had work to do before scrabbling together a dinner for the kids. Not that they couldn't make their own meals, but Aaron felt obligated. Ashley had always cooked dinners for her family. Aaron had been invited to their house for dinner often, back when things were happy and normal.

Aaron shook himself. He couldn't let himself fall into a black hole of despair. No, he could think about other things.

He smiled to himself as he thought of his surprise encounter with his mystery woman. When he'd been visiting Hazel Island earlier in the summer, he'd been walking along the beach when he'd run into her. And against his better judgment, he'd kissed her.

He should've known she wasn't just a tourist he'd never see again. It seemed as though she lived here.

Aaron had met plenty of beautiful, alluring women. He knew how to charm them, how to get them into his bed. But when he'd encountered his mystery woman, his curiosity had been piqued.

"She's not even my type," he groused. Which was true: he preferred leggy blondes. This girl was short and curvaceous. She also had a mouth on her. Aaron got enough mouthiness from his niece and nephew. He didn't need it from any woman he dated.

Aaron didn't have time for dating, anyway. He sometimes had time for a fling or two, but nothing long term. Very few women wanted to become stepmothers, let alone stepmothers to two kids grieving their parents.

Aaron opened his inbox, going through his emails. He'd recently purchased a retail property here on the island, one that was located in a prime spot on the island's main street. It also had ridiculously low rents for its tenants. When Aaron had first seen the amounts, he'd assumed it'd been a typo in the initial email.

He worked until it was close to eight o'clock. He grimaced. So much for making dinner.

"Pen? Logan?" Aaron called outside their rooms, which were just across from each other. "Are you hungry?"

Pen opened her door to say, "We already ate."

"Why didn't you tell me how late it was?"

She shrugged. Pen was tall for her age, nearly two inches below six feet. Sometimes Aaron had to remember she was only thirteen, not eighteen. With her dark blue eyes and sandy brown hair, she also reminded him painfully of Jason.

"I made us some frozen pizza," she explained. "You were busy."

"You know I've told you that I'm not too busy to make you guys dinner."

"I'd rather have frozen pizza than eat your cooking!" yelled Logan from inside his room.

Aaron rolled his eyes. "Did he tell you that he was sent home from school again today?" he said to Pen.

"No." Her eyes widened. "Is he gonna get expelled?"

"That's what I'm trying to prevent." He eyed her. "Do you think you could talk to him? He won't listen to me." Aaron felt guilty for asking, but he was desperate.

"Maybe. He doesn't really listen to me, either," replied Pen.

Aaron felt awkward, standing in the hallway like this. "Can I come in?"

Pen hesitated but eventually nodded. She opened her door to admit him into her little corner of the universe.

Pen loved anime and manga, and her room was covered in posters of her favorite series. Most of the posters consisted of extremely pretty boys with the lead heroine, with an adorable animal or two as well. She had an entire bookshelf filled with volumes of manga. When Aaron had tried asking her about her favorite series, she'd gotten so embarrassed that he hadn't asked her a second time.

She'd painted her walls a bright, cloying magenta, although there were so many posters you could barely see the color under them. Her schoolwork covered her desk, while mounds of clothes were draped on various pieces of furniture. A stack of books looked ready to collapse next to her bed.

Pen sat on her bed and pulled her knees to her chest. In that moment, she looked so young and lost that Aaron's heart twisted.

"May I sit?" he asked.

She shrugged. He'd take that as a yes.

Sitting next to her, he commented, "Did you get more posters?"

Pen nodded. "That one," she said, pointing at one near her desk.

"That's cool. You really like this stuff, don't you?"

He could feel her eye roll. "Obviously."

Aaron felt his palms grow sweaty. When he'd agreed to take in his brother's kids, he'd naively assumed that things would just work out. He'd known the kids since they'd been little. They were family. They'd grieve, of course, but then they'd get along just fine.

Aaron hadn't known how astronomically his life would change, taking in Pen and Logan. It was like someone had launched a bomb into his life and he had only just started picking up the pieces.

"How are you doing?" he asked Pen. He cleared his throat. "Are you okay?"

She gave him a weird look. "I didn't do anything."

"No, no. I know. You're very well behaved. Which is appreciated." He rubbed her hair, which got him another annoyed look. "I just wanted to check in. I know Logan takes a lot of my attention."

"He's always been like that. Even when Mom and Dad were alive."

"Younger siblings do that." His lips quirked. "I probably did the same thing. Your dad had to put up with me getting into all kinds of trouble."

Pen said nothing. Aaron was tempted to leave her alone once more, when she suddenly said, "I miss them." Her voice was small and sad; she hugged her knees more tightly.

"I miss them, too," murmured Aaron.

"I don't get why we had to move away. I liked my school. So did Logan."

"I thought a fresh start would be good for all of us."

"Maybe you were just thinking about yourself."

"You know that's not true. You guys weren't happy in my tiny apartment in Seattle. Here, at least, we can live in a house."

"I didn't mind it." Pen shrugged a shoulder. "At least I still had my friends. Now I don't have any."

"You will. It takes time. And you still talk to your Seattle friends, right?"

"It's not the same."

Aaron knew he was losing this argument. He assured Pen that she'd end up liking her new school, although she remained unconvinced.

When Aaron went downstairs to make himself dinner—microwaved ramen with a few hardboiled eggs—he wondered if Pen were right. Had he uprooted their lives because he'd been running away from his own demons?

He shook his head. They'd needed more space, and that hadn't been affordable in the city.

When he returned to his office, he opened his newest email, his eyes widening as he read it. Then he let out an incredulous laugh. Apparently, the owner of the bookstore he'd just gone to had some balls. Too bad he wasn't about to let them get out of the necessary rent increase Aaron had instituted.

Aaron might be failing in the child-rearing department, but nobody could say he didn't know how to do his job— even if that meant being ruthless at times.

CHAPTER THREE

"This guy is such an asshole!" complained Alex to her friend and new roommate, Felicity Linden. "You should see these emails he keeps sending me. You can tell he does not give a single fuck that he's raising the rent so high."

As Felicity was busy cooking dinner, she only nodded and kept chopping onions. Felicity was kind enough to cook for both herself and Alex on occasion. Although Alex's older sister was a talented chef, Alex hadn't inherited the cooking gene. Her only specialty was peanut butter and honey sandwiches. And takeout—lots and lots of takeout.

Felicity soon handed Alex a plate of orange chicken stir-fry she'd made from scratch. Alex hummed happily as she ate. "You could give Jocelyn a run for her money," she joked. "This is so good."

Felicity ducked behind her blond hair. Her hair was usually in her face, mostly because she was self-conscious about the large wine-stain birthmark that covered the left side of her face from temple to jaw.

Alex had once mentioned that Felicity didn't need to

hide behind her hair, but Felicity had refused to listen. Despite her sweet, shy demeanor, Felicity had a spine of iron when she needed to use it.

"Don't tell your sister that," said Felicity with a smile. "She's way too competitive. She'd probably make us compete to see who's really the best."

"Oh, she'd sabotage you, no question. Jocelyn's ruthless."

After they'd eaten, Alex was once again checking her email. In the past week, she and this Aaron Morrison character had exchanged several emails, each reply getting terser. Aaron refused to budge on the huge rent increase. When Alex had even admitted that the bookstore was struggling, he'd had the audacity to reply, *That's not my problem.*

"It's such a dick thing to say," said Alex as she poured herself another glass of wine. "'That's not my problem'! He could've at least sounded sympathetic."

"To be fair, it isn't his problem," Felicity pointed out.

Alex scowled. "Whose side are you on?"

"No one's. I'm just watching this cage match and trying not to get hit with any flying objects."

Alex laughed despite herself. "I'm not above throwing furniture at this guy's head at this point. Good thing he's in Seattle."

"Please don't get arrested for assault. I'll have to find another roommate then."

"Oh, that's all I am to you? Half the rent?" joked Alex.

Felicity shrugged, smiling. "You said it, not me."

Alex had been living on her own up until the last year, when she'd asked Felicity if she wanted to move in with her to help offset her living expenses. And also because she already knew that Felicity would be an easy person to live with. She was cleaner than Alex, she was responsible, she made sure their utilities were paid on time. All in all, Alex had probably gained more from the arrangement than Felicity had.

Then again, Alex had a feeling, despite her shyness, Felicity longed to be more social. She rarely dated; Alex had never seen her even go on a second date with a guy. If anything, Alex could get her friend out of the house on a regular basis.

Alex's phone alerted her to a new email. Her last reply had amounted to, *It's my problem, sure, but you could also try to work with a long-term tenant who's always paid her rent on time.*

She opened Aaron's latest email, her jaw dropping as she read it.

Looking at the building's records that Stephen gave me, you were late on your rent on five occasions in the past three years. I'd hardly consider that to mean "always."

My offer still stands as is, no matter how many times you email me.

"Five times! My rent has been late once, maybe," fumed Alex. "And it was because I switched banks and things got messed with my automatic payments. Five times, my ass!"

"I wonder where he got that number." Felicity frowned.

"He's probably just making shit up now." Alex downed the rest of her wine, her heart hammering in her chest despite the warmth of the alcohol.

She began typing her reply message, an evil grin forming on her face. When she started laughing evilly, Felicity asked, "What are you doing, Alex?"

"I'm telling him exactly how I feel about him."

"Are you sure that's a good idea—"

Before Felicity could stop her, Alex pressed reply. Her expression was triumphant.

"What did you send?" Felicity took the phone from Alex's hand. Felicity found the email, her face going pale. "Alex, no."

"It's not that bad."

"You called him a selfish dickwad!"

"Did I? I thought I changed that to asshole." Alex shrugged. "It still applies."

Sighing, Felicity returned her phone and then took her wineglass away. "I have a feeling you're going to regret this once you sober up."

"I'm not drunk."

"Tipsy, then."

Now Alex was getting annoyed. "I don't need you to lecture me. This guy was lying about me and using it against me. He deserved it."

Alex knew she sounded like a child in that moment. Redness crept into her cheeks, but soon drained away when she reread the email still open on her phone.

At the salutation—*Eat my ass*—Alex put her head in her hands. "What have I done?" she groaned.

Felicity patted her on the shoulder but said nothing. That was never a good sign when even Felicity didn't have advice.

"I guess you're going to have to pay the new rent," said Felicity eventually. "Or…"

Alex looked up, hopeful. "Or what?"

"You're going to have to grovel. Big-time grovel. More groveling than you've ever done before."

Alex collapsed onto the couch, sighing loudly. "I was afraid you were going to say that."

To Alex's surprise, she didn't receive another reply. She obsessively looked at her email day after day, waiting for the ax to fall. She'd considered calling Aaron and apologizing, but when he didn't reply, she hoped that maybe he hadn't gotten the email after all. Maybe the universe had decided to be kind to her for once.

"Do you have this book?" a girl asked Alex, startling her out of her thoughts.

The girl handed Alex a small piece of paper with a name scrawled across it. Alex's lips quirked. She knew this author well: she wrote steamy historical romance novels. Alex had read every single one.

Alex eyed the girl in front of her. She didn't recognize her. She was tall—almost a head taller than Alex—but she wouldn't meet Alex's gaze. Alex couldn't help but notice that the girl's jeans were too short for her, along with the sleeves of her jacket. Clearly, this girl was constantly outgrowing her clothes, poor thing.

"We have her books," said Alex, returning the slip of paper, "but I'm pretty sure we don't have that one. Let's check, though." She motioned for the girl to follow her.

The girl looked over her shoulder, like she was afraid someone was following her. Or, more likely, she was afraid she'd see someone she knew while she was browsing romance novels.

Alex led the girl to the romance novel section. "Yeah, looks like we're out. I can order it for you, though."

The girl chewed on her lower lip. "I don't have a credit card," she whispered.

"That's okay. Cash works."

"Is it extra if you order it?"

"Nope. I should get it in a week or so. Will that work?"

The girl nodded. Alex took her to the cash register, where she took down her information. *Penelope Morrison.*

Morrison? Surely this sweet girl couldn't be related to that asshole. But wasn't Aaron in Seattle? So it must be a coincidence, she figured.

When Penelope began to wander around the store, Alex couldn't help but follow her. Maybe it was because she knew what it was like to feel like you needed to hide your reading habits.

Although Alex had usually been confident and daring, she'd felt intense embarrassment that she loved romance novels. It hadn't helped that when Jocelyn had found Alex's stash, she'd teased her for months about it. Even worse, Jocelyn had started reading one of the sex scenes aloud in a ridiculous voice until Alex had begged her to stop.

"How long have you been reading romance?" asked Alex.

Penelope hunched her shoulders. "For like a year, I guess."

"Well, if you want some more historical romance recommendations, I can give you some."

The girl's eyes lit up. Smiling, Alex pulled out a few of her favorite authors: Lisa Kleypas, Julie Garwood, Elizabeth Hoyt.

"Lila White is also great, but she writes contemporaries," said Alex. "This one is my favorite. It's an enemies-to-lovers rom-com. I nearly peed myself laughing."

"I haven't read any good rom-coms. The authors that I've read try too hard," said Penelope.

"Or their references are too old for you to get?" teased Alex.

"Pretty much. Who's Brad Pitt, anyway?"

Alex sighed loudly, which made Penelope giggle.

But then the girl's expression shifted to one of surprise. "Uncle Aaron! What are you doing here?" she said.

Alex turned to see a familiar face: her mystery beach kisser. Then her brain registered what Penelope had called him. *Aaron.*

He's Aaron fucking Morrison, Alex thought in dismay.

She nearly sprinted straight out of her own bookstore right then, but it seemed as though Aaron didn't know who she was.

Until Penelope said, "This is Alex. She works at the bookstore."

Aaron's gaze landed on her like a grenade. The tension in the store increased so much that even Penelope seemed to feel it. She kept looking back and forth between them, confusion on her face.

"Alex," intoned Aaron, the sound somehow displeasing when he said it. "Your last name wouldn't happen to be Gray, would it?"

Alex considered lying. She also considered taking one of the heavy hardcovers from the shelf next to her and hitting him upside the head.

Instead, she replied in a tight voice, "That's me."

"Do you two know each other?" asked Penelope.

Aaron smirked. "Something like that."

Alex tipped her chin up. She wasn't going to let this man bully her. No matter if he also happened to be the man she'd kissed on a moonlit beach and hadn't been able to stop dreaming about—

Stop it! That guy never existed!

"Pen," said Aaron, "meet me outside."

"But it's raining."

"Then meet me at the front."

Pen narrowed her eyes, but she eventually obeyed with a huff.

Alex eyed her office door. She'd have to get around Aaron to get to it, but if she succeeded, she could lock herself in there. He'd eventually give up and leave.

But Aaron stepped into her personal space and she found herself neatly cornered. *Asshole.*

"So, you're the one who keeps harassing me via email," he said.

"I could say the same about you."

"You know, I thought I was emailing with a man, based on your name. I had no idea when we met last week that you owned this place."

Alex pulled a face. "Because only a man can own a business?"

"Hardly. It's more that you write like a man."

Alex scowled. Fine, she didn't use exclamation marks in her emails or, even worse, the dreaded *lol.*

"Well, I'm a woman. And I'm the owner of this place. Sorry." She shrugged.

Aaron was still smirking. Alex had never wanted to

smack a man as much as she wanted to smack him. He looked so sure of himself, as if he'd already won their battle.

"You know, I was trying to come up with a reply to your latest email," he began, his smile growing wider, "but now I have the opportunity to tell you in person."

Alex swallowed. "Okay?"

He leaned closer, his breath warm against her cheek. He smelled like pine and salty sea air. This close, she could see the five o'clock shadow forming on his cheeks and jaw.

"What did you say again? Yes, that's right. 'Eat my ass.'" He chuckled. "I'd be more than happy to eat any part of you that you'd like, *Miss* Gray."

Alex's body thrummed. Her nipples hardened.

Before she could make another huge mistake, she pushed him away.

And then, because she was a total coward, she dashed toward her office and slammed the door shut.

CHAPTER FOUR

aron didn't know what possessed him to follow Alex. No, the woman who'd been harassing him over email couldn't be the same woman he'd kissed on the beach. His mind wouldn't accept it.

"Uncle Aaron?" said Pen behind him. "Are you okay?"

He grimaced. He watched as Alex shut her office door, and he was sure he heard the lock click. "Fine," he ground out.

He could feel Pen giving him that look that only teenagers could do, the look that said plainly that he was full of shit.

"Um, I'm going to go get something to eat," she said, "at the coffee place."

"I'll meet you there shortly," replied Aaron as he stalked toward Alex's office.

He didn't even wait for Pen to leave. He knocked on Alex's door and said, "We need to talk."

"No, we don't!" Alex called back.

Aaron breathed in. Then he breathed out. He made

himself think of relaxing things: the waves of the ocean, a meadow. Bunnies and flowers. But then the imaginings turned into him tossing Alex into the ocean, him tackling Alex in a meadow—

"We. Need. To. Talk," he repeated.

Alex opened the door a tiny crack. Now he could only see one skeptical brown eye. "You have my email."

"No. In person."

"You look like you're about to shit a brick."

Bunnies. Flowers. Bunnies. Flowers. "I'm. Fine."

"You promise you won't strangle me?"

He didn't know if he should promise such a thing, but he nodded anyway. When Alex finally opened the door, he moved past her and stood in front of it.

He didn't trust her not to bolt a second time.

Alex raised an eyebrow, her arms crossed. This only made her cleavage more prominent, and Aaron had to tear his gaze away from her breasts.

"Well?" Alex said. "You wanted to talk to me?"

Aaron realized that he didn't really know what he'd wanted to say. He'd been so frustrated with her running off that now he was nonplussed. Or maybe it was just that his brain still hadn't reconciled who she actually was.

He cleared his throat. "I believe our communication has gone sideways."

That made Alex chuckle. "Sideways? It's been drowned and buried at this point."

"I have been nothing but civil to you."

"Raising someone's rent by twenty-five percent is hardly civil."

"That's business, Miss Gray. You are a business owner,

right? Times are tough. Prices keep going up. Your rent was below market. When was the last time your previous landlord raised it?"

He knew the answer to that question, but he wanted Alex to say it out loud. She fidgeted, not looking at him directly.

"He never raised it since I took over the bookstore," she muttered.

"Exactly. Did you know it hasn't been raised in over ten years? Which means that now it has to play catch-up? The amount I'm paying on the mortgage of this building would not be covered with the measly rent Stephen had been charging. It's as simple as that."

"It doesn't make it right!" Alex scowled. "If you had any soul, you'd at the very least raise the rent gradually. I know I'm not the only one who's afraid that I'm going to have to shut my doors. Jackie, who owns the nail salon next door? She already told me she's leaving by the end of the year. She's been here twenty years. How is that okay?"

"As I keep saying, this isn't personal. It's business. I have nothing against anyone renting in this building. But we're not friends. You're my tenant."

"Oh, I know very well that I'm not your friend. And I'm pretty sure you *have* no friends. Is everything in your life a transaction? Because a bit of humanity is not a weakness."

Aaron felt his anger rising again. He could understand Alex's frustration, but at the end of the day, it wasn't his problem. Either she found the means to pay, or she was out. It happened every day. Aaron wasn't going to feel guilty when logic and practicality proved his point.

"You don't know a damn thing about me," he said, his

voice tight. "Now you're just throwing around accusations because you can't get your way."

Her eyes widened. "That's not fair—"

Aaron stepped closer until she had to lean back slightly so their bodies wouldn't touch. The tension in the air was palpable. As Alex licked her bottom lip, Aaron could feel his body heat. He wished he didn't still feel this attraction for this woman. Why had he been so impulsive and kissed a stranger that night?

Aaron was rarely, if ever, impulsive. He lived his life by spreadsheets and numbers, and his relationships had followed similar paths. If a girlfriend did this, he did that. If she said this, he said that.

But he had no formula to understand Alex Gray. She was a complete wild card.

"You're very preoccupied with the idea of fairness," said Aaron softly. "I hate to break it to you, but life isn't fair."

"That's a cynical thing to say."

Aaron thought of his brother and sister-in-law dying and leaving behind their two kids. No, life wasn't fair. He'd known that for a long time now.

"Maybe it's cynical, but I'm not living in a fantasy land," he said.

"It's not a fantasy to want people to treat me with respect like I do already."

"Oh, I respect you." Aaron reached out and tucked a strand of her hair behind her ear. "I respect that you'll do whatever it takes to get what you want. Which, I'd argue, is hardly respectful. If you respected me, you'd respect my decision and work with me, instead of against me."

"There's nothing to work with! You won't even consider a payment plan, or gradual increases—"

He was tired of this conversation. Giving in to impulse once again, he swooped down and kissed her. She protested, pushing at him, but it took all of five seconds for her to melt. As he kissed her, he remembered why he'd kissed her that first time.

Aaron moved his mouth across her lips in soft strokes. His hands on her waist, he could stroke the undersides of her breasts as he stroked his tongue against hers. Alex moaned, her fingers digging into his shoulders.

Then, just as suddenly, Aaron broke the kiss. He stepped back. They were both breathing hard; Alex's nipples were visible under the thin knit of her t-shirt.

"Why did you kiss me?" she whispered.

That made him smile wryly. "To get you to shut up for once."

Alex's expression turned to rage in an instant, and Aaron was ducking as she threw something at his head.

"Get out! Get out of here now!" she yelled.

Dodging another item thrown at his head, Aaron got out of the office and shut the door in the nick of time. He heard the thump of something heavy against the wood and grimaced.

Maybe don't keep kissing women who would gladly murder you, he thought grimly to himself as he went to find his niece.

AARON KNEW he was going to get an earful the second he sat down at the coffee shop with Pen. She'd ordered some iced frothy drink that barely resembled a cup of coffee, her expression trying to appear blank but failing miserably.

Aaron stalled by ordering his own drink. Then standing, waiting for his drink. Then he used the restroom. He was considering getting a sandwich when Pen asked, "Sooooooo?"

"So what?"

Pen made a face. "What was up with you and that lady?"

"It's boring. She's my new tenant. That's the building I recently purchased. That's all."

Pen looked skeptical. Aaron had to restrain himself from fidgeting. Who knew that a thirteen-year-old could make a grown man squirm in his seat?

"You guys were acting super weird," said Pen finally.

"Adults always act weird."

Pen slurped the last of her drink through her straw in one obnoxious noise. "I liked her. She was nice. Before you showed up, she was giving me book recommendations."

"Don't you already have a pile of books at home you should read?"

"Yeah, but you can always add more."

"I thought you only read comics?"

Pen rolled her eyes. "I read more than just comics. Duh."

"My apologies. What kinds of books do you like to read?"

At that question, Pen was the one who started fidgeting. She shrugged, her hair covering her face. "This and that. Depends on my mood."

Considering Pen and Alex had been standing near the romance novel section, Aaron could guess what his niece liked to read. He frowned. Should he let her read books like that? He hadn't even considered that. Pen always seemed so mature for her age that sometimes he forgot that she was, in fact, still a child.

"Is there sex in those books?" he asked.

Pen made a shushing noise, her cheeks turning red. "Oh my God! Don't yell it to the entire place!"

There were all of three other people who were nowhere near their table, but Aaron decided it wasn't worth arguing that point.

"So that's a yes," he said, raising an eyebrow. "You're only thirteen."

"So?"

"So you aren't old enough for books like that."

Pen crossed her arms, her eyes narrowing. "Since when do you care what I do? I'm not the one who's always getting into trouble."

That was the crux of the issue, Aaron knew. He'd been so focused on Logan lately that he'd neglected looking after Pen. Oh, he asked her how her day was, asked her if she needed help with her homework. He kept her fed, clothed, and housed. But he knew that wasn't enough. Guilt made his shoulders slump.

"I'm sorry if I'm not as around for you as you need," he said. He tried to take her hand, but she just tucked both into her armpits. "It's been a hard year for all of us."

"Whatever."

He knew that "whatever" meant *I'm not ready to talk about this* in Teenager, so Aaron decided to let it go. For now.

"I hate living with only boys," said Pen suddenly. Her lower lip wobbled. "I miss my mom. She wouldn't care about me reading romance."

Aaron wasn't sure Ashley would have approved, but she probably would've handled the issue better than he had so far. Some things, he figured, really should be handled by a girl's mother.

"I know you miss her," he said softly.

"Logan is gross. He gets pee all over the toilet seat."

Aaron sighed. "I'll remind him. Again."

"And he smells." Pen wrinkled her nose. "I told him to use some deodorant, and he got all mad at me. Whatever. If he wants to be stinky, he can be."

Aaron hadn't noticed this, either. Or perhaps he'd just assumed preteen boys just tended to stink. Clearly, he was not paying enough attention to the details.

"Once again, I'll talk to him," said Aaron.

"Alex was really nice. She wasn't judgey or anything. What did you do to make her mad? Because I want to keep going back to the bookstore."

"I'm glad she was nice." He had to force himself to say the words, but it was a struggle. Despite himself, jealousy nipped at his heart at Pen's statement. It seemed as though she'd bonded with Alex in one afternoon when Aaron felt like she'd pushed him away in the last year.

"She reminds me of my mom," said Pen, digging the knife further into Aaron's heart.

"Your mom was a lot taller."

"I don't mean she looks like her." Pen shrugged again. "I don't know. She just did."

"When I took you two in, I was worried about being a

single parent. And I know how important having a mom around is right now, especially for you. I mean…" Aaron made sure to lower his voice this time. "You can always come to me, though. If you need supplies or for me to buy you pads or—"

Pen sank down into her chair. "I want to die," she muttered.

"Have you started your period, even? When do girls start them?"

Pen just covered her ears and shook her head.

Alex would know the answer. She'd probably know just what to say to Pen.

He realized in that instant how much Pen—and Logan—needed a mom. Aaron had avoided dating anyone in the last year, but perhaps that'd been selfish of him. What if he could find a woman who'd make a great stepmom to his niece and nephew?

Of course, he'd only marry her if they cared about each other. But they wouldn't have to be in love. Aaron knew too well that love just made things complicated.

Did such a woman exist? Maybe. At least he should start looking for her.

"What if I did get married?" said Aaron.

Pen's eyes widened. "What? To who?"

"I don't know."

"Um, okay."

"I mean, what if I found somebody who'd be a good mom for you and Logan?"

Pen's face screwed up. "I don't want a stepmom."

"Only because you've read too many books where the stepmother is evil."

Pen considered that point. "I mean, maybe. Logan probably would hate it, though."

"You let me deal with your brother."

CHAPTER FIVE

As Alex watched her older sister, Jocelyn, give her husband, Luke, a loving kiss, she couldn't help but find it strange still. Jocelyn had loathed Luke for years until she'd married him suddenly over a year ago. Even then, Alex hadn't been convinced that either of them had married because they'd fallen in love.

Alex didn't doubt now that they were in love. But the image of her sister raging about some annoying thing Luke had done hadn't left Alex's memory, either.

"Why are you making that face?" Luke said, laughing at Alex's expression. "Are we making you nauseous?"

"Oh, you two make me want to puke all the time," she joked.

Jocelyn wrinkled her nose. "No talking about puke when there's food about to be served." Jocelyn gave Luke a pat on his ass and returned to the kitchen.

Alex had come over to their new place for dinner that evening. Her relationship with Jocelyn was better than it had been a year ago, although under the surface Alex could still feel some tension. Or perhaps she was just imagining that Jocelyn disapproved of her still. Alex had been caught in a cycle of resenting her sister for so long that it was going to take time to unravel her own emotions.

Luke Wright was handsome in a rich, preppy kind of way. With his chiseled jaw and perfectly styled hair, he wasn't Alex's type. But she was happy for her sister. Jocelyn deserved a guy who loved her unconditionally. It helped that he was rich, too. His family was the wealthiest on the island. Everyone knew that the Wrights were not a family you wanted to cross.

"So, how are things with the bookstore?" drawled Luke.

Alex instantly thought of her encounters with Aaron and had to stifle a grimace. She doubted her sister or brother-in-law would understand her antipathy toward her new landlord. Or that she'd kissed him before she'd known who he was.

"Fine," she lied.

Luke eyed her. "You know 'fine' is a four-letter word."

"And here I thought you weren't very smart." Alex patted his hand. "Good job."

"You know what I mean. Any time Jocelyn says she's fine, she means the opposite."

"That's because my sister is still terrible about being honest about her emotions," Alex pointed out. "But I'm not."

"No," said Luke dryly, "I'd never accuse you of hiding how you feel."

That comment made Alex chuckle. Where Jocelyn was more self-contained, even cold at times, Alex was impulsive. Fiery. Their opposite personalities had clashed as they'd grown up. It had taken maturity and adulthood for them to be able to see that they were actually on the same side.

Jocelyn popped her head out of the kitchen. "Come get your food," she said.

"What, you aren't serving us?" said Luke.

Jocelyn swatted at him with a wooden spoon as Alex and Luke started filling their plates.

As the head chef of Lyn's Eatery, which Jocelyn co-owned with Alex's other friend Gwen Parker, Jocelyn knew her way around a kitchen. Tonight was roast chicken with Spanish rice and caramelized onions and peppers. Alex inhaled the scents of chili powder and garlic, her mouth watering.

"This looks amazing," said Alex.

Jocelyn preened. "Luke, you should learn from my sister. She knows what to say to a chef."

"Pretty sure you didn't mind what I was saying last night," he said.

Alex squawked, while Jocelyn threatened him again with her wooden spoon. Luke, undeterred, just laughed and headed back to the dining room.

They ate in companionable silence. It wasn't until they were sipping their sangrias that conversation resumed.

To Alex's chagrin, Jocelyn quickly turned it toward the bookstore once again.

"She told me it's fine," said Luke before Alex could answer. He waggled his eyebrows.

"Don't answer for my sister." Jocelyn shot Alex a look that said, *None of this bullshit "fine" stuff.* "Is it really fine?"

Alex decided it was a good time to take a long drink of sangria. And then a second. Jocelyn had perfected the older-sister stare-down when they'd been kids. It took all of Alex's self-control not to become defensive simply out of habit.

"Business is slow," Alex hedged. "But I'm hoping it'll pick up."

"Hope is not the same thing as having a strategy," replied Jocelyn.

Luke leaned down and whispered something in Jocelyn's ear. To Alex's surprise, Jocelyn's expression softened. Only Luke could get her sister to do that. Jocelyn wasn't exactly a soft touch in most circumstances.

"I'm talking to Lila White again. I'm hoping we can try to have a signing with her. She seems interested," said Alex.

Jocelyn frowned. "Didn't she flake on you?"

"She was sick. It wasn't her fault."

Jocelyn didn't look convinced.

Luke said to fill the silence, "She's pretty popular, right? I'm sure she'd draw a lot of people to the store."

"Right? And maybe we could expand to other authors. Not a whole lot want to come here to a tiny island for a signing, but if Lila White starts a trend..." Alex shrugged. "It could work out nicely."

"That's a lot of 'what-ifs,'" said Jocelyn. "But they don't pay the bills."

Suddenly, Jocelyn grimaced. Luke was looking anywhere else but at his wife.

"Well, it probably won't matter anyway. Did I tell you guys that Stephen sold the building? I have a new landlord. And he's raising the rent by twenty-five percent," groused Alex.

Jocelyn and Luke glanced at each other. "Talk about burying the lede there, Alex," joked Luke.

"Twenty-five percent? Are you sure?" asked Jocelyn.

"Completely sure. He refused to budge, too. He says the rent should've been raised years ago so that's why it's so high now." Alex sighed. "Even if Lila White comes to sign and that goes well, it still might not be enough."

Luke frowned. "Who's your new landlord?"

Alex barked out a laugh, which made her sister and brother-in-law give her puzzled looks.

"Aaron Morrison," spat Alex. "The most arrogant, hardheaded, stubborn asshole I've ever met."

Luke was now scrolling through his phone before he showed Alex the screen. "Is this him?"

Alex took Luke's phone to read the article. *Seattle real estate mogul to make his mark on Hazel Island.* At the top was Aaron's headshot, which made Alex scowl. He looked smugly handsome. She wished she could reach through the screen and strangle him.

Alex skimmed the article before returning the phone to Luke. "Yeah, that's him."

"I've met him once before, years ago, back in Seattle. He was an up-and-coming investor at that time. I hadn't realized he'd made his way here, though," said Luke.

"Apparently he lives here now," said Alex glumly.

Luke raised his eyebrows. "Really? I wonder why. Then again, this place has plenty of investment opportunities. All kinds of new construction is going on, tourism increasing—"

Jocelyn poked Luke. "Yes, yes, we can see the dollar signs in your eyes, dear."

"Pretty sure the only person with dollar signs in their eyes is Aaron."

Luke finished his glass of sangria and proceeded to collect everyone else's. "Refills?" He then disappeared into the kitchen.

Jocelyn raised an eyebrow. "So are you going to be honest now?"

"About what?"

"Come on. You and I both know the bookstore isn't doing well."

That statement made Alex bristle. "I'm doing the best I can."

"It wasn't a comment on how hard you've worked. But you and I both know that place hasn't been profitable since you bought it."

It was an argument as old as time. Alex, for one, was tired of hearing about it from her sister.

"How many times are you going to bring that up?" snapped Alex. *Where was Luke with their refills?*

"Until it becomes a non-issue." Jocelyn folded her arms. She looked as unmovable as stone, and it triggered something inside Alex.

"Look, as I've said before, I'm not going to explain my business to you. Maybe it'll fail. Maybe I won't be able to pay my rent. But it's not your business. I'm an adult. I'm not a teenager anymore," said Alex.

"You're acting like one right now."

Alex saw red. Her sister had that *look*—the look that said Alex was silly and immature while Jocelyn was thoughtful and responsible. That if Alex were just mature enough to listen to her wise older sister, her life would be much easier.

Alex took a deep breath. Then another. She clenched her fist under the table and then forced herself to let it go.

"We're getting nowhere with this," she finally said tightly. "I don't want to argue."

To Alex's relief, Luke finally returned with their refilled glasses of sangria. "Arguing? You guys never do that!" he said lightly.

ALEX LEFT her sister's house feeling tired and defeated. Jocelyn had been standoffish for the remainder, until Alex decided she wasn't going to win this round. Even Luke had seemed nonplussed, and it was rare for Luke Wright to have nothing to say.

At five years older than her, Jocelyn had been more of a mother than a sister to Alex when their mom had abruptly left them when they were children. Their dad, Pete, had done his best to raise them on his own, but he'd worked long hours. So it had fallen to Jocelyn, starting at the age of only ten, to make sure Alex had clean clothes, dinner, and her homework completed every day.

But as Alex grew older, she'd begun to strafe at Jocelyn's control. She'd expected Alex to fall in line, and when Alex had rebelled, Jocelyn had come down hard on her younger sister. It had caused a lot of resentment on both sides, something that had nearly destroyed the sisters' relationship when they had been teenagers.

It started because an older boy began flirting with Alex. At fourteen going on fifteen, Alex hadn't dated anyone. Jocelyn hadn't allowed it. But Devon Birch was a senior to her freshman, and he was the most popular boy in school. A football player, he was on track to receive multiple offers to play football in college.

The day Devon slid into a seat next to Alex at lunch, his smile easy and playful, she nearly died on the spot. Ignoring the gaping mouths of Alex's friends, Devon asked Alex a few random questions that eventually led to him asking her out.

Alex barely remembered sputtering an acceptance before Devon sauntered off.

In retrospect, Alex had a feeling that Devon had been interested in her because she'd developed early. With large breasts and curves, she looked like she was older than she was. But she was too innocent to realize what Devon's game was.

He was sweet at first. He showered her with little gifts—a teddy bear here, a box of chocolates there—and took her out on dates. He didn't even kiss her until the third date. But as their relationship progressed, he pushed her boundaries.

A breast squeeze here, an ass grab there. When Alex balked, he told her she was overreacting. All girls did this. She'd liked it.

In a breathless whirlwind of first love that bordered on obsession, Alex fell in deep with Devon. When Jocelyn found out, though, she was furious. Not because dating was wrong, per se, but because Jocelyn was convinced Devon was bad news.

"Didn't you hear what happened with his last girl-friend?" Jocelyn asked Alex one night.

"He told me she was crazy."

"I bet he says that about all of his exes." Jocelyn looked disgusted.

Jocelyn's dislike of the situation only gave Alex more of a reason to rebel. When she grounded Alex, Alex would sneak out. When she took away Alex's phone, Alex bought a burner phone.

If Jocelyn told their dad about the situation, Alex never knew. Knowing Jocelyn, she probably believed it was her duty to take care of things.

It all came to a head when Alex sneaked out on a school night and stayed over at Devon's all night. Jocelyn was frantic, trying to find her. When Alex returned home the following morning, Jocelyn refused to even speak to her.

A few days later, Alex's dance coach took her aside to tell her that she no longer had a spot on the team. Alex loved dance, and she was good enough to get a scholarship.

"Why?" asked Alex, tears falling, sobs making it difficult to breathe. "What happened?"

Her coach seemed hesitant to explain. She only told her that her behavior had not represented the dance team in a positive light.

When Devon was soon investigated for statutory rape, though, Alex realized her getting kicked off the dance team had been Jocelyn's doing. And now Devon could go to prison.

Their screaming fight had nearly brought the walls of the house down. Alex couldn't remember exactly what had been said, beyond her screaming that she hated her sister and would hate her until she died.

Then Jocelyn left to attend culinary school, and it was only until years later that Alex realized Jocelyn had been trying to protect her. Even if it was difficult for Alex to admit that, even now.

Staring up at her ceiling, Alex suddenly felt sick to her stomach. Thinking about Devon did that, though. Where once the thought of him brought butterflies, now it only brought nausea.

Maybe Jocelyn was right, Alex thought sadly. *And maybe she's right about me still.*

CHAPTER SIX

Aaron soon realized that his goal of finding a woman who would make a suitable mother for Pen and Logan wasn't an easy task. He knew it wouldn't be as simple as going to the store to buy a gallon of milk, of course. But as he began making discreet inquiries about available bachelorettes on Hazel Island, he discovered that there weren't many to choose from.

Even worse, one of the most eligible bachelorettes was Alex Gray herself. Aaron would rather drown himself in the Pacific Ocean than pursue her. She'd probably poison him, anyway. He didn't trust her one bit.

So what if he regularly woke up with a hard-on after reliving their kiss, a kiss that would turn into him having sex with her right on the beach? Dreams were just that: dreams. They meant nothing.

Aaron had begun paying attention to moms picking up kids at Pen and Logan's schools, particularly the ones who weren't wearing rings. He felt like a stalker, though, when

Pen caught him one afternoon staring at a blond woman getting into her car, her son getting into the passenger side.

"You're being creepy," stated Pen without preamble.

Aaron snorted. "Thanks, Pen. You always know how to make me feel so confident."

On a beautiful evening in early October, Aaron decided to take a jog along the shore. He used to run all the time in Seattle, but he'd fallen off the wagon since moving to the island.

When he saw a lone woman gazing at the sunset, his initial reaction was to pass her without bothering her. But as he got closer, he slowed, taking in her profile.

She was tall, thin, and blond, her hair so pale that it looked white. She was wearing an oversized hoodie and sweats that concealed any possible curves she might possess.

Aaron racked his brain, trying to remember if he'd seen her before. He'd probably passed her on the street. The island was small enough that everybody knew everyone else's business.

The woman looked up. Aaron was startled when he saw that she had a large, wine-stained birthmark on the left side of her face.

She quickly covered that side of her face with her hair. Based on the blush that covered her other cheek, she probably rarely let strangers see the left side of her face.

Guilt hit him a moment later. He hoped she hadn't seen his expression change at that revelation. She was a pretty woman regardless, and he found himself interested in her more for this very detail.

Even better, she didn't have a ring on her finger.

"Did I startle you?" said Aaron, shooting her an easy smile. "Sorry about that."

The woman was staring at her shoes. "It's fine."

She didn't volunteer any more information. Based on how she was playing with the strings of her hoodie, she was uncomfortable.

"I'm Aaron Morrison," he said, offering his hand. "I'm new to the island. I don't think I've seen you yet."

Her right eye widened. "Oh. Um. Hello." Aaron's hand was still outstretched, and she finally took it the same moment Aaron brought his arm back to his side.

Their fumbling made Aaron chuckle. The woman, though, just blushed harder.

Aaron put his hand out a second time. "Let's try that again. I'm Aaron."

The woman's lips turned upward in a hesitant smile. "I'm Felicity." She finally took his hand, and they laughed.

Aaron was able to coax Felicity into telling him a little bit about herself. She was a freelance writer, she worked from home, and she'd lived on the island since her early twenties. When he asked her what kind of writing she did, she told him it was mostly helping people with their resumes.

"I should send you mine," said Aaron.

"I thought you worked for yourself?"

"If it gave me the excuse to see you again, I'd do it."

Felicity looked away, but Aaron could see that she seemed pleased. When he casually asked her about her boyfriend, she quickly assured him she had no boyfriend.

It didn't take much longer for Felicity to give him her number. Then he told her goodbye and continued his jog along the beach, hopeful that his plan was coming to fruition.

~

THE FOLLOWING SATURDAY, Aaron sat on the heated deck of Lyn's Eatery with Felicity for their first date. Although she was wearing a sweater and jeans this time, her sweater was at least two sizes too big.

Normally, Aaron didn't care what anyone wore, but he found himself annoyed that Felicity hid her figure even on a date. He suppressed those thoughts quickly. *She isn't a flashy person*, he reminded himself.

Besides, this wasn't about attraction or chemistry. This was about seeing if she'd make a suitable mother figure for his niece and nephew. Aaron couldn't be selfish in this regard.

Unwittingly, he remembered how Alex had felt in his arms. How she'd kissed him with such unbridled enthusiasm that just the mere memory made his body tighten.

"Something wrong?" asked Felicity, breaking through his thoughts.

He gave her a tight smile and reassured her that all was well.

"So how did you get into resume writing?" he asked after they'd eaten their appetizers.

"I just fell into it. It pays the bills."

He waited a beat, hoping she'd expand. But she just nibbled on the last bite of garlic bread, her gaze on her plate.

Aaron sighed internally. He considered buying Felicity

another drink to get her to relax, but she didn't seem like much of a drinker.

He asked her more questions about her work, her family, her hobbies. Although she would answer, she didn't ask him questions in kind. Aaron didn't know if that meant she was uninterested, or she just didn't know how to hold a conversation.

When Felicity mentioned that she liked doing jigsaw puzzles in her spare time, Aaron tried to come up with some pithy comment. But all he could think to himself was that activity sounded beyond boring to him.

He was close to calling it a night, but he forced himself to keep trying. Clearly, Felicity was shy. Who knew how much dating experience she had? Maybe if he were patient, things would improve.

This isn't about you, he reminded himself.

When they received their entrees, it gave Aaron a moment to collect himself. He couldn't look at this like his usual hookup, where he'd gauge it successful if he felt chemistry with his date. The women he hooked up with weren't shy wallflowers like Felicity. They were confident in their sexuality, flirting outrageously with Aaron while he responded in kind.

Aaron understood women like that. Women like Felicity? They were a mystery to him.

After they'd both finished their meals, silence reigned. Felicity looked like she wanted to melt into her chair.

"Are you having a bad time?" asked Aaron suddenly.

Felicity's eyes widened. "What? No. Why would you think that?"

"You just don't seem like you're enjoying yourself, that's all. We can call it a night if you'd like."

"Are *you* having a bad time?"

Aaron considered saying yes, but he didn't have the heart to be mean to her. He'd been the one to ask her out, after all.

"We don't have a lot to talk about," he said instead. "Surely you've noticed."

Felicity played with her hair. "I'm not good at this." She gestured vaguely. "Um, dating, that is. I'm not good at talking to strangers. Especially guys. Sorry."

Aaron's frustration melted away. Taking Felicity's hand, he squeezed it. "I thought as much, but I couldn't tell if it was because you were shy, or just didn't like me."

"I don't know if I like you." She blushed when Aaron laughed. "I mean, I don't know you yet. That's all."

Aaron was about to reassure her when the last woman in the world he wanted to see approached their table. Alex had a sickly sweet smile on her face, her gaze solely on Felicity.

"Liss, you didn't tell me *this guy* was your date!" Alex poked Felicity in the arm.

Felicity hunched down. "Um—"

"Do you two know each other?" asked Aaron.

Alex laughed. Her cat-like eyes swiveled toward him, and it felt like an arrow straight to his gut. "Oh, she didn't mention that we're friends? And roommates?"

Aaron felt absurdly betrayed, even though it was ridiculous. What did it matter who Felicity was friends with?

"Based on your face, you had no idea." Alex grinned evilly. "I just wanted to say hello. Don't mind me."

"Obviously, we're minding you." Aaron's voice was tight.

"He's probably mad that he has to pay for dinner," Alex said to Felicity. "He's kinda weird about money. Knowing him, he'll invoice you later for your part of the dinner."

Aaron wondered why strangulation had to be illegal when people like Alex Gray existed in this world.

Felicity, at least, looked annoyed at her friend. "I'll see you back at home," she said firmly.

"Now I've made Felicity mad. That's never good." Alex scowled over at Aaron. "If you do anything to hurt her, your balls are mine."

Aaron stood up, throwing down his napkin. "That's it! You've insulted me more than enough this evening!"

"It's not an insult if it's true!"

As he and Alex bickered, Aaron barely noticed Felicity getting up and saying quickly, "I'll meet you at the front."

Aaron knew they were already attracting attention. After paying the bill with cash, he took Alex around the back of the restaurant where there was some modicum of privacy.

"Did you come down here to ruin my date?" he accused. "Because it's none of your damn business who I go on dates with."

"Wooooow, seriously? You really think I care that much about *you* that I'd try to sabotage your date?" Alex looked incredulous. "I didn't even know you were the guy Felicity was seeing! I was getting some things at the store and saw you guys eating."

"And then you had to come over and make a scene."

"Protecting my friend from an asshole like you? Yeah, I'll fucking make a scene!"

"You are the most frustrating, obnoxious, meddling woman—"

"Those sound like compliments to me."

Aaron wanted to tear his hair out. He also had the urge to pull on Alex's hair like some kindergartener.

"Listen to me," he hissed, pointing a finger in her face, "leave me alone. If I want to date every single one of your friends, I will. I'll come over to Felicity's place and you'll listen to us having sex and you won't say a damn *thing* because it's none of your goddamn business!"

They were both breathing hard now. Although he'd been talking about Felicity, an image of him and Alex having sex burst into his mind. It didn't help that Alex's breasts were straining the buttons of her blouse, or that she kept licking her lips, or that her face was as red as he'd imagined it would be when he thrust inside her.

He grabbed her before he realized what he was doing. He kissed her hard, and she gave as good as she got. He felt the wildness in himself mirrored in her. He grabbed at her ass, at her hair; he squeezed her breasts and thrust his tongue into her mouth at the same time.

Alex moaned, panting now. Aaron was as hard as a rock. He wondered if he could drag her inside and fuck her right then.

"Um, hello? Oh dear," said a female voice close by.

Alex jumped away from him at the same time Aaron shoved her away. It took a moment for his brain to compute that the owner of Lyn's Eatery, Gwen, was staring at them both with an amused expression.

"Well, this just made my night more interesting," mused Gwen. A pretty redhead, Gwen looked like she belonged on a dairy farm, what with her creamy skin and freckled cheeks.

"I need to go," blurted Alex. She didn't even look at Aaron as she hurried away.

Aaron didn't know what to say. Did he explain? Did he lie? Did he just leave?

"The food here was really good," he said desperately.

Gwen's lips were twitching. "Thank you. I'll tell the chef," she said seriously.

"I'll have to come for brunch some time."

"You should."

Aaron waited another beat. Then: "I should go."

"Probably a good idea. I'll see you later."

Although she waited a few seconds, Gwen's laughter soon followed him all the way to his car.

CHAPTER SEVEN

"Why did you go out with him?" Alex demanded when she returned home.

Felicity was currently doing dishes. Glancing over her shoulder, she replied calmly, "Because he asked me to."

Alex wanted to throw something. Mostly, she wanted to clobber Aaron Morrison until he begged for mercy.

How dare he kiss her right after he told her he'd date her best friend? The man was a sadist. He probably didn't have a soul.

Felicity finished the dishes and was wiping her hands on a dishtowel as she watched Alex pace across the length of their small dining room.

"Why would you go out with a guy like that? You know he's been a huge asshole to me!"

Felicity sighed. "I mean, according to *you*, he's been an asshole. But there's always another side to a story."

Alex stared, incredulous. "You're seriously taking his side?"

"I'm not taking anyone's side! You guys can have your tiff or whatever this is if you want. But he was nice to me, he asked for my number, I decided it'd be nice to go out for once. That's the end of it."

Felicity headed to the living room and collapsed into the overstuffed brown chair that she and Alex tended to fight over all the time. More than once they'd gotten into pillow fights when somebody stole the chair when the other person went to the bathroom.

"He's a dick," said Alex. "He's raising the rent on the bookstore. And I kissed him!"

Felicity frowned. "I'd forgotten about the kiss. Do you still like him?"

"Obviously not!"

"Then what's the problem?"

Alex struggled to explain. She also knew she was probably being a huge hypocrite, considering she'd just kissed Aaron a second time tonight. *He kissed* me, she reminded herself. *That kiss was his fault, not mine.*

If her brain reminded her that she'd kissed him back, Alex decided to ignore that small detail.

"You're *my* friend. Not his. Friends are loyal. Even if you think this thing is stupid, you should have my side," said Alex.

"I told you, I'm not on anyone's side!"

"Well, you obviously don't believe me and think I'm being overdramatic."

Felicity just shot her a wry look. "You sound jealous, you know. If you want me to stop seeing him, I will. You know that."

Alex knew she was cornered. Admitting that she might

still be attracted to the man she also happened to loathe was too much. Her pride wouldn't let her. Swallowing hard, she just looked away and scowled.

"I thought as much," said Felicity.

"You don't get it. Why can't you just do this one thing for me? Aren't we friends?"

Felicity sighed. "Alex! Listen to yourself right now! You're being selfish."

"Me? Pot, meet kettle!"

"Look, unless you tell me you want to date him, then you forbidding me from seeing him makes zero sense." Felicity suddenly looked sad. "Do you know the last time someone asked me on a date? Three years ago. It went so well that he never contacted me again." She huffed a bitter laugh. "I'm not exactly getting offers. Not with my face."

Guilt made Alex's shoulders slump. Going to the couch near Felicity, she said, "You're gorgeous. You know that."

"Most guys don't see past my birthmark. It's fine. I'm used to it. But sometimes it's nice when a guy looks at me without staring like I'm some freak."

"I didn't realize… You never talk about it."

"Because having people pity me is the worst." Felicity wrinkled her nose. "Although considering how our date went, I doubt Aaron will want another. It was a disaster, even before you showed up."

"I doubt it was a disaster."

Felicity recounted her date, proving that it had, in fact, not gone well. Alex couldn't help but appreciate that, despite the subject being painful, her friend could still maintain her sense of humor.

"I'm sorry," said Alex meekly. "He just gets me riled like nobody else I've ever met."

"Even your sister?"

Alex chuckled. "Okay, Jocelyn does that, too. But it's different."

Felicity's smile was sly. "Because you don't go around kissing your sister?"

By the end of the night, they were friends again. As Felicity talked about how exciting it was to have a guy as handsome as Aaron ask her out, Alex realized that she was being selfish.

She didn't want Aaron. She hated him. But couldn't she set aside that feeling if her best friend wanted to date him?

Her stomach turned at the thought, but Alex knew it was just because she disliked him. *Or that you're not telling Felicity about that second kiss.*

"I'm just so bad at talking to strangers," said Felicity as they drank tea in the kitchen before bed. "I get so stuck in my head and end up saying either something stupid or nothing at all."

"Did you tell Aaron that?"

"I was trying to, when you showed up."

Alex winced. "Sorry."

"Like I said, he probably won't contact me again. So all of this is probably making a mountain out of a molehill." Felicity looked thoughtful now. "Did you know his niece and nephew live with him? He mentioned it briefly."

"I knew there was a girl, but not about the boy."

"He asked me later if I'd ever thought about having kids. It was a little weird. Who asks that question on the first date?"

"A weirdo, that's who."

Felicity shrugged, smiling a little. "Or he wants to find a mom for them."

"How Victorian of him," was Alex's wry reply.

As the week began, Alex watched Felicity look at her phone constantly, her disappointment clear on her face. When Aaron didn't contact her by Friday, Felicity shrugged and said she'd figured as much. But Alex could tell that Felicity was hurt.

The scheme came to Alex's head during those strange times in the middle of the night, when you wake up for a few minutes and wild ideas spring from your head like Athena from Zeus.

And when Aaron came into the bookstore that Saturday with Pen, Alex knew she had to act.

AARON GAPED AT ALEX, and then he started laughing. "You can't be serious."

"Do I look like I'm joking?"

He considered her, his brow furrowed. Even frowning, he was handsome, the sunlight bringing out the golden threads in his hair. He was cleanly shaven this morning, and Alex had the sudden urge to rub her fingers along his jawline and cheeks.

"You want to help me date your friend," repeated Aaron. "Why? What's in it for you?"

"Felicity is my friend. I'm doing this for her."

He barked out a laugh that made Alex scowl. "No way

in hell. You're not doing this for her. You're doing it for yourself. Don't try to convince me otherwise."

"Well, I'm not doing it for myself as the *main* reason," she hedged.

Aaron just waited and drank his coffee.

When Alex had asked Aaron to meet her in a park not far from Main Street on Sunday morning, she'd naively assumed he'd accept her offer without question. He wanted to date Felicity, but Felicity was a hard woman to get to know because of her shyness.

Alex could coach Felicity while also giving feedback to Aaron on Felicity's interests. She'd act as a coach and mediator.

"Fine." Alex sighed. "I want you to lower the rent on my building."

"Now I know you're joking."

"Hey, it's a 'you scratch my back, I'll scratch yours' deal. I'll help you and Felicity to get to know each other. Or I'll help you find another woman to date. In exchange, you increase the rent gradually over the course of a few years."

Aaron was shaking his head, his expression amused. "You are brazen, I'll give you that. Although I never thought you'd use your friend for your own gains."

"I'm not using her when she wants to go out with you." At Aaron's surprised look, Alex chuckled. "See? You assumed she wasn't interested. She is. She's just shy."

"And she's okay with you doing this?"

Alex studiously did not look Aaron in the eye.

"Brazen," he muttered. "So fucking brazen."

"Do you want my help or not?"

"You're assuming I *need* your help."

"Based on how your first date went, you do." Alex paused, then added, "Felicity mentioned that you asked her if she wanted kids someday."

Aaron tensed. "Yeah, so?"

"That's a bit intense of a question to ask on the first date."

"I was curious."

"Or," said Alex as she slid closer to Aaron, "you were interviewing her to see if she was okay with you already having kids. And maybe to see if she'd be okay becoming a mother eventually to them."

"That seems a stretch." Despite Aaron's words, he looked a bit like he'd been caught red-handed.

"Look, I don't care what your motives are, as long as they aren't evil," said Alex. "If you want a governess, or a wife, or just a girlfriend, that's on you, buddy. As long as you tell Felicity what's up. Don't lead her on."

"I wasn't planning on it." Aaron's voice was like gravel.

"Good. Then think about what I said. I'll help you, you'll help me, and we both make Felicity happy."

"You're forgetting one minor detail. I've already kissed *you*—twice." Aaron's eyes darkened.

Alex realized she was sitting way too close to him. She scooted as far away as she could from him. Being that close to him was overwhelming to her senses. Why had she gotten so close to him in the first place? *Like a moth to a flame.*

"So? We don't like each other. Those kisses were just a random thing."

"Maybe the first, but not the second."

Alex swallowed. Aaron's expression was predatory, and she had a feeling if they weren't surrounded by other park-goers, he'd pounce and make her his. The memory of their second kiss behind Lyn's Eatery filled her mind.

"Tell me you aren't attracted to me," he commanded.

"I'm not attracted to you."

She said the words so quickly they were barely intelligible. Aaron laughed.

"Sure, sweetheart." He rose and stood over her. "You keep telling yourself that when you're thinking about me and touching yourself."

"I am not thinking about you when I'm doing that!"

"Thank you for confirming that you touch yourself." He touched her jaw. "Now I'll have something to keep my brain occupied."

Alex stood up, but he was so close that the backs of her knees were pressed against the bench, and there was barely an inch between their bodies. She could feel his heated breath on her face.

"Don't you dare think about me," she hissed. "Not if you're dating my friend."

His smile was smug. She wanted to kick him in the knee right then.

"You don't sound so sure," he mused.

"I'm completely sure. Don't think about me. Don't imagine me. Don't even say hello to me on the street."

"I thought you were going to help me?"

"I'm helping Felicity!"

His lips twitched, and then he stepped away. Alex let out a breath.

"You just keep telling yourself that," he repeated.

"Is that all you can say to me? I'll tell myself whatever I want." Grabbing her own coffee that had been sitting untouched, she was annoyed to find that it was already cold. She'd blame that on Aaron, too, the ogre.

"I'll talk to you later then?" he asked.

She huffed in annoyance. "Fine. But I won't be looking forward to it."

CHAPTER EIGHT

Aaron knew he was in for it during a parent-teacher conference when Logan's sixth-grade teacher, Ms. Dean, looked at him over her glasses and just sighed heavily.

"Mr. Morrison," Ms. Dean began, "you're aware of your son's behavior lately, I'm sure."

"He's my nephew."

"Well, you're his primary guardian, correct?"

Aaron nodded. He'd resisted taking on the title of father for Logan and Pen because it felt like a betrayal to Jason. Jason was their dad, not Aaron. Aaron was just the replacement that didn't quite fit.

"Logan is obviously a smart kid. Too smart, probably," said Ms. Dean.

"Can someone be too smart?"

"When school isn't difficult for certain kids, they can act out. Although I have a feeling Logan isn't acting out just because he's bored." Ms. Dean made a note on her pad that

Aaron desperately wanted to read. "How are things at home?"

Aaron considered if he could lie. But he had a feeling Ms. Dean could see a lie from a mile away. And she'd call him out and put him in the corner.

"It's been touch and go," replied Aaron.

"I ask that because there's a direct correlation between how well a student does in school and how their home life is. I know Logan has been through a lot in the last year, and this is a new school and new classroom. But he's disruptive to the other students. It's not fair to them when Logan acts the way he does."

"Are you talking about the incidents in the cafeteria? And in PE?"

"Not just those. He pesters his classmates. He tries to write on the backs of their necks. He tied one girl's pigtails to her chair. He passes notes constantly, no matter how many times he gets caught. It's gotten to the point that I've had him sit by himself in the back away from the other students."

Aaron swallowed. "I wasn't aware it was that bad. I can talk to him. I mean, I will talk to him. It's not okay that he acts like that."

"Do you see that kind of behavior at home?"

"Not to that extent. He tends to stay in his room when he gets home. I try to talk to him, but he won't let me."

Aaron felt lost. Most of all, he felt angry with his brother for dying. *I can't do this. Why aren't you here?*

As Ms. Dean provided Aaron with more examples of Logan's rowdy behavior inside the classroom and out of it, Aaron struggled not to get defensive. His teacher seemed fixated solely on Logan's negative traits with little to say about anything else.

"Maybe something's wrong with him," said Aaron. "Maybe I should take him to a doctor."

"You can, but I've seen kids like this before. Generally speaking, they need someone with a strong hand to keep them in line."

Aaron gritted his teeth. "He's a kid."

"He's old enough to know better."

"We're doing the best we can. *I'm* doing the best I can."

Ms. Dean clicked her tongue. "I'm sure you are," she said, her tone patronizing. "But I have to tell you that if Logan's behavior doesn't improve, I won't allow him back inside my classroom. I'm sorry. But as I said, it's not fair to my other students."

"So you're just going to give up on him? Is he that expendable?"

"I'm not the parent. You are." She made another note on her pad. "Perhaps you need to ask yourself if you're the best person for the job."

Aaron sat there, stunned. He didn't know if he was more horrified or angry. Horrified, because he wasn't about to re-home his niece and nephew like a couple of puppies. Angry, because he was afraid this woman was right.

"I'd like us to work together to help Logan." Ms. Dean handed Aaron a packet. "Read through those, and then we'll set up another meeting to discuss your nephew's progress."

Before Aaron left, he said, "I might not be the best person for this job, but I took in Logan and Pen because they're family."

"I know that, Mr. Morrison. I wish you the best of luck. I really do."

WHEN AARON KNOCKED on Logan's door the next evening, there was no answer. Aaron knocked again.

"What?" Logan called from the other side.

Aaron jiggled the doorknob. Locked. "Logan. I need to talk to you."

"Not now."

"Yes, now. Open this door."

Aaron waited, wondering if he was going to have to find a way to unlock the door himself. Finally, Logan opened the door, a scowl on his face.

Sometimes it hit Aaron hard how much Logan looked like Jason: the same eyes, the same stubborn tilt of the chin. Logan, though, was still baby-faced; he hadn't yet hit puberty, so he looked younger than he actually was.

Aaron wrinkled his nose when he shut the door behind him. Logan's room was a pigsty, and it smelled like one, too.

"Logan, it stinks in here," said Aaron, going to the window and opening it for some fresh air.

Logan shrugged and returned to the overstuffed chair he sat in to play video games. "I don't smell anything."

"Probably because you're used to it. Are you remembering to wear deodorant at school?"

"Um, sometimes."

Considering the stick of deodorant that Aaron had given Logan months ago was still mostly full, Aaron knew that *sometimes* really meant *never*.

"I had a meeting with Ms. Dean last night," said Aaron.

Logan just continued playing his latest video game.

"Logan, listen to me."

When his nephew continued ignoring him, Aaron turned off the console and then began to unhook it.

"Hey! You can't do that!" Logan leaped up and tried to push Aaron away.

Aaron, though, wasn't going to be deterred. He hadn't taken away his nephew's video games because, in all honesty, he hadn't wanted to deal with the arguing. But he realized he needed to step up his game.

"I'm taking this because of how you've been acting at school. You'll get it back when you prove you can behave," said Aaron.

Logan's face was turning red. "That's not fair! I didn't do anything!"

"You're going to be kicked out of your class. What happens if you get expelled?"

"I don't care!"

"I know you're angry about your parents—"

"It's not fair! It's not fair!" Logan was crying now, and he curled up in his chair, sobbing.

Aaron felt guilty, but he knew he couldn't give in. He set the console near the door and then sat across from his nephew.

"Buddy, I need you to work with me here. How can I help you?"

"Go away. I hate you." Logan's face was buried in the depths of the chair's cushion.

"That's a mean thing to say."

"It's true."

Aaron sighed. His tone firmer, he said, "You need to stop acting up in class. Ms. Dean told me that you're distracting the other students, keeping them from learning. How is that fair for them?"

"Ms. Dean sucks," was Logan's mumbled reply.

"She's your teacher. You need to be respectful."

"She keeps putting me in the back of the class, even when I don't do anything. She hates me. It doesn't matter what I do."

"She doesn't hate you."

Logan's expression was mulish. "You don't get it."

Aaron had a feeling Logan was correct on that score. But he wasn't about to admit it. "How you're acting is not okay. If you keep acting up, you'll keep losing privileges. TV, going to your friends' houses—"

"Shut up! Go away!" Logan's was close to screeching now.

"Tell me to shut up one more time, and you won't get to watch TV for a week."

Logan decided to remain silent after that declaration.

Aaron closed himself in his office, feeling like the weight of the world was on his shoulders. Worst of all, he was so frustrated with Logan that he was afraid he'd say something he'd regret. How did a kid manage to get under his skin so easily? Had he ever been that rude to his own parents?

HAZEL ISLAND MIDDLE SCHOOL was a small school. There were only two teachers per grade. If Logan was placed in the other class and was kicked out, they'd be screwed. Aaron knew he couldn't homeschool. He had his own work, and he knew he wouldn't make a good teacher.

Looking at the photo of his brother and his family, Aaron said bitterly, "Why did you leave us? I don't know if I can do this."

Jason kept smiling, and so did Ashley. Pen and Logan looked so young in the photo, and happy. Aaron hadn't seen those expressions on their faces since their parents had died.

It had been a day like any other when the accident had occurred. The entire family had been in the SUV, driving home from Pen's band recital, when a drunk driver had hit them head-on.

Ashley had died instantly. Jason had been flown to the hospital and had died the next day. Miraculously, the kids had survived with only some scrapes and bruises.

Aaron went to his brother's side as soon as he'd heard, and he was with him when he'd died. It was the worst day of Aaron's life when his brother had died. He was sure a huge piece of himself had died with him.

Jason had been three years older than Aaron, and Aaron had always looked up to him. When they'd been kids, Jason had looked out for Aaron. When Jason had hit puberty, he'd started hanging out only with his friends, avoiding his geeky younger brother.

Aaron had been a late bloomer. He'd been short, awkward, and pimple-faced until his last year of high school. Jason, though, he'd been popular in school. When he'd started dating Ashley in high school, Aaron had watched from afar, envious of his older brother.

But when puberty had hit Aaron with a vengeance, Jason had been away at college. When he and Ashley had gotten married and soon had kids, it was only then that Aaron and Jason reconnected.

Aaron had enjoyed being the fun uncle. He remembered when Pen and Logan were little and sweet. They'd demand rides on Aaron's shoulders until his neck ached. When he brought them candy on one occasion, they never failed to search in his pockets to see if he'd brought them candy again.

Jason and Ashley had been amazing parents. Even Aaron, who knew nothing about parenting, had seen that. Aaron had been amazed to see his usually hotheaded older brother become so patient with his kids. When they threw tantrums, Jason had rarely lost his cool.

Ashley had been the homemaker, the nurturer. She'd kept their house immaculate. Aaron had never seen a single speck of dust anywhere in that place.

Aaron picked up the framed photo. The grief, he'd realized, ebbed and flowed. Some days, he felt almost normal. Other days, though, it felt like he could barely breathe.

Sometimes, he'd wake up in the morning and forget that Jason was dead. But then it'd hit him in a rush, and it was like getting that call from the police all over again.

Staring at that family photo, Aaron realized that he needed to work harder on giving the kids a mother. Ashley could never be replaced, but they needed more than Aaron could give. If that was Felicity, then he'd date her and marry her. It didn't matter if she wasn't the woman of his dreams.

Despite himself, he thought of Alex. His grip tightened

on the frame. He knew her "deal" was probably a trap. That woman only cared about pleasing herself. But if she could get Felicity to feel more comfortable with him? It'd be worth putting up with that devil woman.

CHAPTER NINE

Felicity gaped at Alex. "You can't be serious."

"Why wouldn't I be?"

"You hate Aaron. This would help him. Why would you do anything that would help *him*?"

Alex tried to keep her expression neutral, even as she wanted to scowl.

When she'd told Aaron that she hadn't mentioned her plan to Felicity, her guilt had pressed on her. She should've mentioned this to Felicity first.

Which meant she wasn't going to tell her friend that she'd spoken with Aaron already. Alex figured that in this instance, ignorance was truly bliss.

"I'm doing it for you," said Alex firmly. "You looked so sad that he never texted you again that I wanted to do something about it."

"I'm not sure you giving me a Cinderella makeover is going to change anything."

That made Alex laugh. "I'm not giving you a makeover, unless you want one. I just meant being a go-between for you two. A mediator. A helpful third party who's completely neutral."

Felicity snorted. "Yeah, right. Neutral."

"I will be!"

"You are the biggest liar. But I have to admit, I'd like to see you try."

Gwen Parker stepped up to their table with a smile. "What is Alex trying out now?" she asked, pulling up a chair. As the co-owner of Lyn's Eatery, Gwen was either at the restaurant or at the bed-and-breakfast next door.

Alex felt herself blushing when Gwen shot her an amused look. *She clearly hasn't forgotten about finding me and Aaron kissing.*

Alex suddenly realized she'd been a complete idiot to have this conversation with Felicity at Gwen's restaurant. Gwen would have questions. A lot of questions, ones that Alex wasn't at all prepared to answer.

"Alex wants to help me with dating," said Felicity, her nose wrinkling.

"Oh, really? Since when did you become a dating coach?" asked Gwen.

"I wouldn't call myself a coach. I'm a third party that can give each person feedback. That's all. Kind of like a matchmaker. Wouldn't it have been nice if your granny could've told you that Jack was actually into you when you had no idea?" Alex raised an eyebrow.

Gwen smiled. Her diamond ring winked in the sunlight. After being friends with the grumpy fisherman-turned-carpenter for five years, Gwen and Jack Benson had started a relationship that had quickly transformed into love. But Alex couldn't help but wonder if they would've gotten together sooner if they'd simply been aware of the other person's feelings.

Gwen shrugged. "It definitely would've made things less complicated. You're also assuming Jack would've said a word to my imaginary granny. He's not exactly all about sharing his feelings." She rolled her eyes. "Getting him to write his own vows for our wedding is, apparently, a monumental task."

"I could help him," offered Felicity.

"That's sweet, but he'd never take you up on the offer. Men and their pride," said Gwen.

"I didn't know you were writing your own vows," said Alex.

"I thought it'd be fun. But I guess I was just thinking about myself." Gwen looked a little guilty. "Whoops."

Gwen and Jack had begun planning their wedding a few months ago, although it wouldn't happen for another year. Gwen, though, she liked to be prepared. Alex knew she'd be the type to procrastinate and come up with something minutes before the ceremony.

Despite herself, Alex imagined herself walking down the aisle. And who was at the end, waiting for her?

Aaron Morrison.

Alex nearly fell out of her hair. She must've looked stunned, because Felicity asked, "What is it?"

"Nothing, nothing." Alex let out a forced laugh. "I was just thinking about how I'd probably be like Jack if I had to write my own vows."

Alex was able to keep Gwen distracted with wedding talk for a bit, but Gwen was too damn savvy. She eventually came around again to the subject of Felicity dating again.

"Is there a guy you have in mind?" Gwen asked with a smile.

"Aaron Morrison. The new guy in town. I already had one date with him," replied Felicity.

Gwen's eyes widened as her gaze swiveled to Alex. Before she could reply, though, Alex kicked Gwen under the table and mouthed, *Say nothing.*

It was fortunate that Felicity had turned to ask the waiter for a coffee refill right in that moment. Gwen, for her part, just narrowed her eyes at Alex, a look that definitely warned her she'd grill her about this subject later.

"I've met him briefly," said Gwen. She was pointedly not looking at Alex when she added, "I've heard through the grapevine that he's a player, though."

Alex clenched her fist under the table.

Felicity's eyebrows went up. "Really? How would anyone know? He's brand new to town!"

"Sweet summer child, have you never heard of social media?" said Gwen.

"Just because he was a player doesn't mean he still is." Alex glared at Gwen. "He could've turned over a new leaf. He has kids, too. That changes a guy."

"A leopard can't change its spots," muttered Gwen.

Alex lightly kicked her. Gwen kicked her back, making Alex jump.

"Are you guys playing footsie?" Felicity joked.

Gwen's smile was sharp-edged, aimed straight at Alex now. "Something like that."

Felicity left to go work on her latest writing project, leaving Alex to contend with Gwen. The restaurant started getting busier, prompting Alex to ask, "Don't you have to go back to work?"

"I'm the owner. I can do what I want."

"I doubt my sister would agree."

Gwen just leveled a stare that made Alex fidget.

"Alexandra Gray, what are you doing?" asked Gwen.

"What do you think that I'm doing?"

"I think you're going to get yourself into another scrape and then act surprised despite being warned against it."

Alex bristled. "That's not fair. I'm helping our friend. That isn't a 'scrape.' You make it sound like I'm an idiot."

"Of course you aren't an idiot. But I saw you kissing the very man you want our friend to date. Don't you think Felicity should know that?"

Alex looked away. "No, because it doesn't matter. That kiss was an anomaly."

"Uh-huh. You guys were about to rip each other's clothes off if I hadn't come outside."

"I was pushing him away."

At that, Gwen's expression softened. "Seriously? Then—"

"Just drop it. Trust that I know what I'm doing. But please don't tell Felicity you saw me and Aaron kissing. It's not worth starting drama over."

Gwen didn't look convinced. Alex was given a reprieve when Jocelyn came out to find the two of them talking.

"Dinner prep is about to start and I'm missing two staff," she said to Gwen. "Help?"

"We'll talk again later," said Gwen quietly before she followed Jocelyn to the kitchen.

Alex told herself that she was doing this because she

wanted to help Felicity. *And the added bonus is that it'll help my bookstore.*

Did that make her an idiot? Maybe. But it was better than sitting on her hands and hoping for the best.

~

ALEX SMILED to herself as she watched Felicity and Aaron from a dark corner. She hadn't told them she'd be there for their second date. They would've been too self-conscious. She'd stay for a little while, and then she'd leave.

If anyone noticed a woman in the corner wearing an overlarge hat and big sunglasses inside a burger joint, they were too polite to say anything. Alex's waitress gave her a strange look, but it was hardly out of the ordinary for tourists to wear something similar.

Alex could just hear what Aaron was saying, although Felicity's voice was too soft for her to make out. Aaron laughed at something Felicity said and touched her arm.

Alex's plastic fork snapped in her fist. She quickly hid the pieces in her purse. A woman across from her raised an inquisitive eyebrow, but Alex ignored her.

"I was never good at writing," Aaron was saying in between bites of French fries. "Did you always like writing?"

Felicity replied with something Alex couldn't hear. To Alex's frustration, Felicity still had her hair in her face to hide her birthmark. She'd also disregarded Alex's advice to wear something a little more daring than jeans and a big sweater.

"I don't like to wear tight clothes," Felicity had said

earlier that day as she'd been getting ready. "I'll be afraid of something falling out all evening."

"It doesn't have to be a crop top and miniskirt. Just a little cleavage," Alex had urged.

Felicity hadn't replied, even when Alex had set out a few of her own tops for Felicity to try on. When Felicity had left their apartment wearing the exact outfit Alex had despaired of, Alex had made the impulsive decision to follow her best friend.

As Aaron leaned more closely to Felicity, his smile warm, Alex realized that she might've made a tactical error. Watching the man she'd kissed—twice—flirt with her friend made her irrationally angry.

You don't even like him. Why do you care?

She had no idea. It made zero sense. It wasn't like she wanted Aaron Morrison for herself.

Aaron's gaze swiveled, finding hers. Alex quickly looked away. She hoped he hadn't recognized her.

Alex asked for a to-go box for her own burger that she'd barely touched and headed out. Her heart was slamming against her ribs, and she wondered if she was coming down with something. She felt sick to her stomach. Or maybe the two bites of hamburger just weren't agreeing with her.

"Do you always stalk your friends?"

Alex jumped, her to-go box tumbling to the ground. Fries and burger spilled across the pavement.

Growling, she snapped, "You scared me!"

Aaron didn't look contrite. He did, however, help her pick up the food and toss it into a nearby garbage can. "I didn't mean to scare you. Sorry about your food. Do you want me to get you another one?"

"No, it's fine. I wasn't hungry anyway."

Aaron's amused smirk had faded to something that looked suspiciously like concern. "You okay?"

"What? Yes. Of course. I'm going home now. Why are you out here?"

"I told Felicity I left my wallet in my car. So I'm sure she's wondering where I am."

Alex felt strangely tongue-tied. It didn't help that the setting sun brought out the gold in Aaron's light brown hair or that he looked especially handsome in his blue polo shirt.

"Then you should go back inside," said Alex, rather lamely.

"Why are you here, anyway?"

"I wanted to see how Felicity did."

"Does she know that?"

Alex grimaced. "No. And don't tell her, please."

"Not sure how you can give feedback on seeing something you weren't meant to see."

"I'll figure it out." Alex shrugged. "Not sure she'd take my feedback, anyway. I told her to wear something sexier than a huge sweater, but she refused."

Aaron chuckled, looking back at the restaurant. "Someone who can tell you no? That gives her lots of extra points in my book."

"Lots of people tell me no!"

"And how many of them do you listen to?"

"Only the ones who are right."

"So, no one?" Aaron grinned, but it faded quickly. "I should go back inside."

"Yeah, you should."

Aaron hesitated, and Alex had the sudden urge to ask

him to go with her. She didn't know where; she just couldn't bear that he go back to Felicity.

But she bit her tongue and smiled tightly, telling herself what she wanted in this instance didn't matter. She had a bigger game plan than getting hung up on some guy who didn't care about her.

Alex watched Aaron return inside. She had the sudden wish to follow him, to return to that corner and watch the entire date from start to finish. Which clearly meant she was a masochist. What would she gain by doing that?

Alex's stomach rumbled. Of course, *now* she was hungry, and there wasn't anything good at home. Alex locked her car up again and headed to Lyn's Eatery. At the very least, she could bum some food off of her sister if she didn't want to wait for a table.

Lyn's was packed, with people waiting outside to get a table. Alex slipped through the back door instead. Jocelyn didn't like when Alex did this, but Gwen wouldn't mind.

As luck would have it, Alex ran into Jocelyn first. Her older sister was red-faced and sweaty, her usual tight bun already starting to fall down. Her chef's uniform was stained with what looked like tomato sauce. Considering that Jocelyn was usually immaculate in her dress and work, there must've been some mishap earlier.

Jocelyn narrowed her eyes when she spotted Alex. "What are you doing here? You know you're not allowed back here."

Alex snagged a dinner roll and took a large bite. "I'm hungry."

"Then order some food like everyone else."

Jocelyn's sous chef, Naomi, grinned. "There's a take-out

order that wasn't picked up over there. Steak and potatoes. You can have it if you want."

Jocelyn shot Naomi an annoyed look. "Don't encourage her!"

Alex let out a happy squeal and snagged the take-out order before Jocelyn could. "Naomi, you're the best. I knew you'd pull through. I got food over at Hamburger Harry's, but I dropped it."

"You dropped it? Are you that clumsy?" Jocelyn asked with a cocked eyebrow.

Alex wrinkled her nose. "Somebody scared me and I dropped it."

Jocelyn looked skeptical, but her attention was snagged before she could comment.

Alex warmed up the steak, potatoes, and roasted asparagus and pulled up a chair to eat in the tiny break room of the restaurant. A baseball game was on the TV in the corner. Alex knew that was Naomi's doing, not Jocelyn's. Jocelyn hated baseball. She must really like this latest sous chef if she put up with having baseball playing on the break room TV.

When Alex finished her meal, her stomach near to bursting, Jocelyn came into the break room and sat down across from her.

"Bad night?" asked Alex, glancing at her sister's stained uniform.

Jocelyn sighed. "There might've been an exploding pot of spaghetti, let's say that."

"You look like you murdered someone."

"Thank you," said Jocelyn wryly. Then she scowled at the TV in the corner and grabbed the nearby remote, changing the channel to a cooking show. "I fucking hate baseball."

Alex laughed. "You almost hate it to an unreasonable degree."

"It's boring. Nothing happens. It's just people standing around. I don't get the appeal."

"Well, thanks for the free dinner."

Jocelyn's gaze shifted back toward Alex, and Alex felt it like an arrow through the gut. "Gwen mentioned that you're doing matchmaking now."

"Gwen has a big mouth."

"Was it supposed to be a secret?"

Alex fidgeted. "No, not exactly. But I'm not advertising it, either. Besides, it's not matchmaking. I'm just helping Felicity, that's all."

"Helping her date the same guy who's raising the rent on your building." Jocelyn sat back, an eyebrow raised. "Now, that's a strange coincidence."

"What are you saying?"

"I'm just asking what you think you're doing."

Now Alex was frustrated. "Why are you grilling me about this? It's not a big deal."

"I'm just worried you're going to get yourself mixed up in something that you'll regret."

"Even if I do," said Alex through gritted teeth, "I'll deal with it."

"Just like you're dealing with your business that's always been in the red? Come on, Alex. Be reasonable."

Alex stared at her sister, incredulous and angry. "You always throw that in my face any chance you get. Yeah, maybe it was a bad idea to buy the place. You've said that a million and one times. I get it. I really do. You think I'm a fuckup and an idiot—"

"I'm just worried about you."

"You're worried that I'm going to make your life harder. It's not about me. It's about *you*."

Jocelyn's face shuttered. "That's not fair and you know it."

A year ago, Alex had had to tell Jocelyn that she was struggling to help with their dad's expenses. Disabled and recovering from a second stroke, Pete Gray had had to rely on his daughters for the past few years. It had only been Jocelyn marrying Luke that Pete had been able to hire a full-time nurse so Pete didn't have to go into a nursing home.

"I know that Gwen saw you and this Aaron guy kissing," said Jocelyn, "and so I'm just confused why you'd want to set him up with Felicity."

"It was a one-off thing. It's not a big deal." Alex's voice sounded strangled.

"If you say so." Jocelyn's tone implied that she didn't believe Alex one bit.

"Look, I hear what you're saying. I know what I'm doing. You don't have to keep acting like you're my mom. I want a sister, not a mother. Okay?"

Hurt crossed Jocelyn's face. Alex was too frustrated to feel guilty over it.

"I need to get back to work." Jocelyn stood up. "Be sure to bus your dishes before you leave."

Alex rolled her eyes. "Yes, Mother," she said under her breath after Jocelyn had left the room.

CHAPTER TEN

Aaron threw himself into his work. He owned a half dozen buildings and was looking to continue to expand on Hazel Island. Despite the island's small size, there were new buildings going up all the time that were great investment opportunities.

One of those buildings would be on land owned by the Wright family and handled by the eldest son, Luke. Aaron had met him on one occasion years ago, never realizing that his family owned a substantial portion of the island itself.

When Aaron had discovered that Luke was also Alex's brother-in-law, though, he'd seriously considered looking elsewhere. But the building was on the main street where most of the tourists visited during the idyllic summer months. It would not only include businesses on the lower level, but apartments above it. Aaron could practically see the money flowing in if he could get his hands on it.

Aaron met Luke at a coffee shop one morning. Luke was friendly as they shook hands, and Aaron let his guard down within a few minutes of their meeting. He'd nearly expected Alex to pop out somewhere and ambush him.

"We're still financing a percentage of the construction," Luke was explaining, "but due to unforeseen circumstances, we'd like to add another investor in. Preferably someone who would also manage the building and the tenants."

"You don't hire a management company to do that?" asked Aaron.

Luke sighed. "Let's just say it's been a challenge to find one worth the money."

Aaron knew that all too well. He used a management company for some of his properties, but for the ones like Alex's building, it was easier to cut out the middle man.

"Given how many units this place is going to have, I'd probably still hire out that work," said Aaron.

Luke shrugged. "Better you than me."

As Luke explained how much it would all cost and what he wanted in terms of Aaron's investment, Aaron asked his own questions. What plans were there to advertise the building to potential tenants? What kinds of businesses did they want moving in? What types of apartments would they be? Would they be only for rent or would they be condos people could buy?

After they'd talked for nearly an hour, Luke said, "I have to say, you've been the most thorough of anyone I've talked to about this."

"When it comes to money, I'm always thorough."

"I believe you. That makes you a smart man." Luke assessed him. "Maybe even a little ruthless, or so I've heard."

Aaron didn't react. He scrawled additional notes on a pad of paper, deciding how he should respond, if at all.

"Sometimes business isn't nice," said Aaron finally.

"You don't have to tell me that. You think my family is where it is now because they were bleeding hearts?" Luke snorted. "No, I'm not judging you for it. But I'm sure you've made enemies, too. I know I have."

"If someone is mad, they can leave a review online."

Luke laughed, so loudly that a number of people in the coffee shop turned to stare. Wiping his eyes, Luke said, "I like you. I probably shouldn't, though. Better not tell the family."

Aaron's curiosity got the better of him. "Your wife is Jocelyn Gray? The chef?"

"Indeed. And her sister is one of your tenants." Luke's expression was wry. "I can commiserate. Alex can be a handful. Then again, so can Jocelyn. The Gray sisters are something else. That's probably why I fell in love with my wife in the first place."

The memory of kissing Alex flashed across Aaron's memory. He knew without a shadow of a doubt that Alex would be firestorm in bed. Just the mere thought made him want to groan.

"I've met Alex," hedged Aaron. "She has a lot of opinions."

"A lot? That woman is relentless. I'm sure she hasn't let you be since you dared to raise her rent."

Aaron's eyebrows shot up. "She told you?"

"She might've mentioned it. She might've also mentioned that you were basically the most evil guy ever. But I haven't seen any devil horns yet."

Aaron chuckled. "No tail, either."

"Both sisters are fighters, to the point that they tend to be their own worst enemies." Luke's expression turned serious now. "I should also warn you that Jocelyn is extremely protective of her younger sister."

"I'm not sure what that has got to do with me."

"Just a bit of friendly advice. If you happened to be interested in Alex—"

"I'm not." Aaron swallowed. "I mean, I'm dating someone else. You probably know her: Felicity Linden."

"Oh, really?"

"You sound surprised."

Luke shrugged. "Alex seems more your type."

Aaron blinked, then he laughed. "You don't even know me. Are you trying to play matchmaker? Is that your new career move?"

Luke looked abashed. "Sorry. My wife must be rubbing off on me. She loves to meddle in people's lives."

"Just like her sister," muttered Aaron.

Luke finished his cup of coffee, tapping a pen against the table. "Look, I'll just say this once. If you're a good guy, you won't mess around with Alex. She's more fragile than you'd think. She acts tough, but a lot of it is just a mask."

"Pretty sure I just told you I'm dating her friend." Aaron could barely keep the frustration from his voice.

"There might also be rumors floating around… Well, you get my point. Just a friendly warning."

Luke's statement was anything but friendly at that point. Aaron had a feeling that if Jocelyn didn't cut off his balls, Luke would finish him off if he so much as laid a finger on Alexandra Gray.

"Well, good thing Alex isn't my type," Aaron said through clenched teeth. "I'd rather not have you break my kneecaps."

Luke didn't laugh. "And I'd rather not have to break them."

~

WHEN AARON PICKED up Felicity for their third date, he made sure to give her flowers with Alex watching in the background. Mostly, he wanted these rumors that Luke had mentioned put to rest.

He also wanted to make sure Alex knew there wasn't anything between them. Those kisses? They wouldn't happen again.

But as Felicity thanked him for the flowers and went to put them in water, he couldn't help but watch for Alex's reaction. She sat at the dining room table, looking at her tablet, completely ignoring what was happening around her.

"Look, Alex! Aren't they pretty?" Felicity placed the vase of flowers on the table in front of Alex. "How did you know that I love chrysanthemums?" she asked Aaron over her shoulder.

"A little bird might've told me," he said with a smile.

Alex had a smile on her face now. When he caught her gaze, though, she looked back down.

"Only you would like something like chrysanthemums." Alex poked at one of the flowers, a deep violet color. "Whatever happened to liking roses?"

"Roses are cliche. Besides, chrysanthemums are in season," replied Felicity.

"Where are you guys going for your date?" Alex played with the flowers; she brought them closer to smell them and made a face. "They don't smell like anything. What's the point?"

Felicity shot Aaron a look that said, *Ignore her.*

Aaron, unable to help himself, said, "Are you saying you wouldn't want any flowers that didn't smell? Because I'm not a gardener, but that rules out a lot of them."

"Isn't the point of flowers to make your house smell nice?" replied Alex.

Her chin was jutted out, and Aaron had the absurd urge to take hold of it and kiss her.

"Sometimes it's just nice to have something pretty to look at," he said. Although he tried to sound lighthearted, the statement wasn't without heat. Especially as he was looking straight at Alex.

A blush crawled up her cheeks. "Why do I get the feeling you aren't talking about plants now?"

"Aaron? You ready?" said Felicity from the doorway.

Felicity's voice nearly made Aaron jump. Abashed, he muttered goodbye to Alex and took Felicity's arm, getting out of their apartment as quickly as possible.

As they ate dinner, Felicity was quiet. Too quiet. Aaron instantly felt like a total jerk. He shouldn't even have spoken to Alex. Had Felicity thought they had been flirting?

He was tempted to say something, but he decided it might make things worse. He also wasn't sure Felicity would believe him if he protested too much.

Felicity said suddenly, "Why do you keep going on dates with me?"

Aaron nearly dropped his fork. He coughed, feeling his cheeks heat. "Why would you ask that?"

"Because you don't seem interested in me. Not really."

Felicity was hiding behind her hair, her gaze on her plate, but he could tell she was upset. *I've seriously fucked up.*

"I'm just…" He sighed, trying to think of something that would make things better. "I'm rusty at this."

Felicity shot him a disbelieving look. "You? Are you telling me you've never dated before?"

"Of course not."

"Then it's me."

He wanted to groan aloud. "No, I'm just not used to women like you." Realizing how that sounded, he added quickly, "I mean, women who are shy. Quiet. I'm used to women who won't stop talking."

"You're used to women doing most of the work."

Aaron wondered where these claws had come from. Felicity had come off as such a scared little rabbit, yet she was more like a house cat deciding it'd had enough already.

"I didn't mean it like that." Aaron took a long drink of his water, wishing he'd ordered liquor instead. "Look, I'll be honest with you."

Felicity raised an eyebrow. "So you haven't been honest?"

"I've left some details out. You know about my niece and nephew? I took them in after their parents died. My brother and sister-in-law. They're thirteen and eleven, and Logan— he's the eleven-year-old—isn't doing great in school. I don't think I can raise them by myself."

Felicity watched him, and Aaron had a feeling there

were many layers underneath her shy exterior that he couldn't begin to understand.

"I started dating again," he continued, "because if I could find a woman who would want me and want to help two kids who desperately need a mother..." He shrugged. "Maybe it was a stupid idea. But they need a mom. Pen, especially. She's thirteen. Girls that age need their mom."

"They need them, but they won't admit it," said Felicity softly.

"Pen is mature for her age. I forget how young she is. Whereas Logan is the opposite. He acts out no matter what I do or say. I can't get through to him."

Aaron realized he was babbling. "Sorry, you don't need to hear all about my personal problems. This is hardly a great topic for a date."

"Maybe not, but I appreciate you being honest." Felicity looked at her hands. "I don't know if I'd make a good step-mom. That's a lot to expect of anyone. But I can tell how much you love your niece and nephew. That you'd do anything for them."

Aaron swallowed hard. "I would. And I do like you, Felicity. I want to keep getting to know you."

She smiled. "I feel the same way."

At the end of the date when Aaron helped Felicity out of his car, he put his hand on her waist and gazed into her eyes. She shivered.

"Are you cold?" he asked softly.

"A little."

"Then I'll warm you up."

He kissed her, the kiss sweet and gentle. She was hesitant, uncertain, but he guided her through the kiss.

When they parted, he saw movement at Felicity's window, a flash of red. Alex had been wearing red earlier. His stomach twisted.

Why did it feel like he'd betrayed a woman he didn't even *like*?

He forced the feeling away. This obsession with Alex? It'd fade—it just had to.

CHAPTER ELEVEN

When Alex sorted books in the backroom, Chris poked his head in to say, "Your buddy is here."

"My buddy? Suzie's corgi?"

Chris snorted. "No, not a dog. The teenage girl who keeps coming around. You know, the super tall one who's always hunched over, staring at her feet?"

Chris spoke in a low tone, although Alex still shushed him. "It's hard being a teenager," she admonished him.

"Oh, you think I don't know that? I was literally stuffed into lockers in high school, like some John Hughes movie."

"Seriously? You fit into a locker?"

"I was a scrawny kid." Chris flexed his bicep. "Good luck getting me into one now."

Alex rolled her eyes, smiling despite herself. "I'm sure Malcolm appreciates the effort."

"Gotta keep my man happy, duh."

Alex forced herself to finish the task at hand before she went out to talk to Pen. Pen had dropped by the store three times now, and Alex could tell the girl had wanted someone to talk to.

God knows having only Aaron as a parent would be hard as a girl, thought Alex. *He probably would freak out if she asked him to buy her pads.*

Alex snickered to herself. The mental image of a sweaty, awkward Aaron going down the feminine hygiene aisle, trying to find the right kind of pad amidst hundreds of choices? She would pay a lot of money to see that.

Alex found Pen browsing her favorite section of romance novels. Her backpack was so full, though, Alex didn't know where she'd store any more books.

"Doesn't your back hurt?" asked Alex, eyeing the backpack. "That thing looks like it weighs twenty pounds."

"It probably does." Pen handed it over to Alex to hold.

Alex nearly fell over. "Holy crap! What are you carrying in there? Bricks?"

"Textbooks are heavy." Pen gave Alex a look that told her that her question was a silly one.

"I thought you kids used tablets now."

"Oh, we do for some things, but the school doesn't want to spend money if it doesn't have to." Pen shrugged. "So we carry around heavy books a lot. My uncle always tells me that his backpacks were way heavier when he was in school."

"Did he also walk five miles uphill in the snow to get to school?" said Alex wryly.

Pen gave her a strange look. "It doesn't really snow much in Seattle, which is where he's from."

"No, I mean—" Alex shook her head. "Never mind.

Generational gap, I guess. So, how are things? With your uncle, that is?"

Alex told herself she was only asking because she had taken a liking to Pen, not because she was still fixated on the guy. It didn't help that she'd had the delightful experience of watching him kiss Felicity after the latest date.

"He tries, I guess. But talking to him is weird. You know when adults try too hard to be cool? Like that," said Pen.

Despite herself, Alex felt her heart soften toward Aaron. "At least he's around. My dad wasn't when I was your age because he was always working."

"What about your mom?"

"She ran out when I was five."

Pen's eyes widened. "Oh, sorry. That sucks."

"It did. But me and my sister got through it."

"My parents died, you know."

Pen was browsing the romance novels as she said the words, in the same tone someone would describe the weather.

"I heard that. I'm so sorry," replied Alex softly.

"Me and my brother were in the car when we got hit. I don't remember the accident, though. I remember asking my mom to turn up the radio and then I was in the hospital. It was weird."

Alex stared at the girl, aghast. She hadn't known the kids could've just easily died, too.

"How terrible," murmured Alex.

"I wasn't hurt that badly. They were afraid about a head injury, but I was fine. My brother, too. But the car that hit us hit us head-on. My mom died instantly, they said. My dad died before I woke up in the hospital."

Alex felt tears spring to her eyes. The recital of bald facts recounting the tragedy was heartbreaking. No thirteen-year-old should have to go through such a tragedy.

"How are you doing now?" asked Alex.

Pen shrugged. "Everyone likes to ask me that. But I don't really know the answer. Some nights I cry myself to sleep, but other days are like any other. Sometimes I get really angry that they died. It's not fair."

"No, it's not."

"Uncle Aaron is always asking me that question. He tells me constantly, 'You can talk to me.' And I guess I could, but what's there to talk about? My parents are dead. They won't be coming back. So we just have to move on."

"I don't think you can move on from something like that. Grief is complicated." Alex smiled sadly. "I acted out a lot, I think, because my mom left. My dad wasn't around and my sister tried to be my mom, but I resented her for it. But I wasn't old enough to understand why I was acting the way I was."

"Logan is like that, I think. He keeps getting into trouble. Uncle Aaron is always focused on him. It's annoying." Pen pulled one of the titles from the shelf, reading the back blurb. "Have you read this one?"

Startled by the sudden change in subject, it took Alex a moment for her brain to recalibrate. The romance was one with a fake-dating scenario. "I've never been a big fan of the fake-dating thing," admitted Alex. "Like, who does that in real life?"

"I'm sure some people have." Pen sounded doubtful. Then her eyes lit up. "Actually, there was somebody at my school who tried to do that. Her ex-boyfriend wouldn't leave her alone, so she asked another boy to act like her boyfriend."

Alex's lips twitched. "In junior high? Seriously?"

"I mean, it didn't work. She got back together with her ex anyway." Pen's expression took on a dreamy look. "Gus has been single ever since."

"Do you like him?"

Pen turned scarlet, then hissed, "No! No, he's weird. He plays the tuba."

"If you really like him, you should ask him out."

"I could never do that. What if he says no?" Pen shook her head. "No way. I'd die."

"You wouldn't die. I promise."

Pen looked skeptical, which made Alex have to keep from laughing. But these kinds of things were extra serious when you were an adolescent. Alex remembered well how intensely she'd thought she'd loved Devon.

The thought of Devon made Alex's stomach twist. "How old is Gus?" she asked Pen suddenly.

"Um, fourteen? He just had a birthday."

Alex forced herself to smile. "Sorry. Ignore me."

THAT EVENING, Alex went over to her dad's for dinner. Jocelyn had been living with Pete until she and Luke had gotten married a year ago. Pete had had two strokes in the past decade. It was only with the help of Luke that Jocelyn and Alex had been able to hire a nurse so Pete could continue living in his own home.

"They were out of crab rangoon," said Alex as she set

out the Chinese takeout she'd brought over. "I got us eggrolls instead."

Pete made a face. "Did you ask if they had any in the back?"

"What, like a secret stash of crab rangoon? No, they were out of crab, apparently. Or that's what Mike told me."

"Mike? He always gets my order wrong. Any time there's something missing, I look on the receipt, and guess who's listed? Mike." Pete shook his head.

Mike was all of eighteen, and he had a tendency to be a bit of an airhead. Alex had learned to repeat her order very slowly whenever he answered the phone at the Sichuan Dragon. Alex had a feeling his only hobby was smoking an inordinate amount of weed during his time off.

She and Pete ate their dinners in silence, *Wheel of Fortune* playing in the background. Pete watched the game show every evening. He'd always say throughout Alex's childhood that he'd go on the show someday. But since his health had declined, he'd stopped saying it.

"What's up, sweetheart?" asked Pete, wiping his mouth. His salt-and-pepper eyebrows merged together as he frowned at her. "You're quiet. Too quiet."

"I'm quiet sometimes!"

"You're only quiet when you're upset. Spill. Is it your sister again?"

Alex hesitated. She always felt guilty mentioning Devon when talking with her dad. He'd had little idea of what had been going on in his own house, and even to this day, he didn't know the full story.

Alex knew her dad would blame himself. What made things complicated was that, logically, she knew he should shoulder some of the blame. He hadn't been around as a parent. But on the flip side, she hated hurting him and wanted to protect him.

She decided to tell Pete about Aaron raising the rent on the bookstore and how he refused to work with her on it.

Pete's frown deepened. "Are you going to have to close the place?" he asked bluntly.

Alex poked at her leftover fried rice. "I hope not. I'm trying not to think about it."

"What happens if you do? What are you going to do?"

"Get a job somewhere else?" She shrugged. "I might have to leave Hazel Island, if all else fails. The jobs here aren't exactly plentiful."

"You know I'd help you if I could." Pete squeezed her shoulder. Then he said softly, "Have you asked your brother-in-law?"

Alex flinched. The thought of begging Luke for money —and in turn, Jocelyn—would be too much for Alex's pride to handle.

"I don't want Luke to think I'm after his money," she said.

"Nothing wrong with family helping family."

"He's not my brother. He's just married to Jocelyn. I wouldn't feel comfortable asking him."

"So, then what? You hope this Aaron guy decides to be kind? That's not much of a plan, sweetheart."

Alex slumped into her chair. "I know. I'm just hoping him dating Felicity will make him more inclined to be nice to me." She crossed her arms over her chest, her heart twisting. "Although I doubt it. He's hardly Prince Charming."

"I thought you only emailed him."

Alex flushed. "We've met in person a few times," she hedged.

"Alexandra Claire," said Pete sternly, "what are you hiding? Spill it."

Alex wasn't about to tell her dad about kissing Aaron Morrison or how she'd been dreaming of those kisses for weeks now. Instead, she muttered, "It's nothing. We flirted. Now he's dating Felicity. The end."

"You don't sound happy about that."

"I'm perfectly happy about it. I'm the one who got them to this point, in fact."

Pete looked confused. "What does that mean?"

"It means I played matchmaker. Kind of."

"For a man you *flirted* with?" Pete's emphasis on the word flirted made Alex's blush deepen.

"Yeah, I did. We never dated. He's not mine. And Felicity deserves a good guy."

"I thought you said he was a—and I quote—'a greedy asshole.'"

Alex scowled, and she threw a balled-up napkin at her dad. "You don't need to quote me!"

After they'd finished *Wheel of Fortune*, Pete said quietly, "Do you know what you're doing?"

"Does anyone?" Alex replied lightly.

"Just be careful. You have a tender heart. I've seen it hurt before. I don't want it to happen again."

Alex felt stupidly close to tears. Why was she being so emotional lately? "My last heartbreak was when I was a teenager. I'm not that girl anymore."

"No, but you fall into things headfirst. Don't avoid

looking around you just because you want to prove something, okay?"

ALEX RETURNED HOME to find Felicity aglow with happiness. She showed Alex the text message she'd gotten that night from Aaron. Apparently, he'd asked her over for dinner to meet his niece and nephew.

"Wow," said Alex, suddenly wishing she hadn't eaten so many eggrolls. "That sounds serious."

"I think he might be the one." Felicity giggled and covered her face. "I'm acting like a teenage girl. It's ridiculous."

Alex felt like she was drowning. She wished she'd never come home. "I'm happy for you," she choked out.

Felicity hugged her. "Thank you. It's all because of you."

CHAPTER TWELVE

On an unseasonably warm day in October, Gwen, Jocelyn, and Alex decided to spend the day at the beach, along with seemingly the rest of the island. Felicity was sick at home with a bad cold. Alex had felt guilty leaving her, but she'd urged Alex that she'd be fine on her own.

Alex stretched her legs, basking in the sun. Families played in the water, while others built sandcastles as best they could with the rather rocky sand. The beaches tended to be covered in driftwood as well, which was great for bonfires but not so great for lying out in the sun. Despite that, the trio cleared a spot and settled in for some much-needed relaxation time.

"I brought libations," said Gwen, opening the giant cooler she'd lugged with her. Inside were a variety of sparkling waters, beers, and wine coolers.

Jocelyn pulled out a beer. "I need a drink. Or five."

"I'd need a drink being married to Luke, too," joked Alex.

Although Jocelyn was wearing sunglasses, Alex knew her sister was rolling her eyes. "My husband is just fine. I'm talking about work."

"Anything new?" asked Gwen as she opened her own bottle of water.

"No, same shit, different day. Why did I say yes to being the head chef again?"

Gwen laughed. "Because you love to be in charge?" at the same time Alex said, "Because you're super bossy?"

Jocelyn harrumphed. "I plead the fifth."

The women talked, read, and drank the afternoon away. Alex couldn't remember the last time it was this warm in October, but she appreciated that the weather was giving them one last warm day before the cold and rain arrived. Although she loved Hazel Island, she'd always disliked its winters.

"Alex!" Pen scampered over. She was covered in sand, her hair wet from the ocean. "Hi!"

Alex smiled, shading her eyes as she gazed up at the teenager. "You went swimming?"

"Duh. We're at the beach."

"It's way too cold for swimming. Especially in a swimsuit. You should tell your uncle to get you a wetsuit."

Alex felt Jocelyn nudge her. She introduced Pen to Jocelyn; Gwen had already met her, apparently.

"Are you here alone?" Alex couldn't help asking herself.

"No, Uncle Aaron and Logan are down that way." Pen waved vaguely. "I didn't want to wait for them. They're slow."

Despite their supposed slowness, Aaron and Logan found Pen after a few minutes. Alex couldn't help but notice that, after Aaron had realized who Pen was talking to, he made a point to look anywhere but at Alex.

After more introductions, in which Aaron barely spoke more than three words to Alex, the kids soon got bored and returned to the waves.

Aaron didn't go with them. Instead, he stood over the trio, his arms crossed.

"Felicity isn't with you?" he asked Alex.

"She's sick."

Based on his expression, she hadn't mentioned that to him. *Interesting.* Then again, Felicity hated being fussed over. When Alex had made her some soup earlier, she'd nearly refused to eat it.

"Is it serious?" he said.

"Just a cold, I think."

Aaron didn't say anything after that. Alex wondered why he was still standing around at all. She was about to tell him he could go when Gwen said to Jocelyn, "I have to pee. Will you go with me, Joss?"

"What, are you going to get lost?"

But Jocelyn finally agreed, leaving Alex to gaze up at Aaron's forbidding figure. He looked like he'd just eaten a lemon.

"Do you want something to drink?" Alex offered. "We have plenty. Probably for the entire beach."

"I'm fine."

When his gaze moved from her, Alex couldn't help but admire the figure he cut. Wearing only swim trunks, she could see that he worked out, his six-pack gleaming with whatever sunscreen he'd put on. He'd already started tanning, which Alex thought was deeply unfair. She was lucky if she could just avoid a bad sunburn.

He looked like some golden god that'd emerged from the waves to kidnap her and make her his mermaid queen. Alex shivered.

"Are you cold?" said Aaron. His gaze moved from her face to her chest, where Alex realized her nipples were hard.

Because she couldn't help herself, she made a point to adjust her bikini top. Then sitting up, she pressed her breasts together, creating some remarkable cleavage.

And Aaron noticed. Oh, he definitely noticed.

"I'm not cold," she said, smiling wickedly. "Not sitting in the sun like this."

He swallowed hard. Then he muttered something about the kids, and he was stalking away. Alex bit her lip, barely containing a laugh.

But then she felt guilty. Here she was, flirting with the guy who Felicity was dating. *They're not in a relationship, exactly*, she told herself, but it didn't help.

She wrapped her arms around her knees, watching Aaron splash Logan and Pen. Logan jumped on Aaron's back, Aaron soon tossing the boy into the water.

She felt herself getting up on the excuse that she wanted to dip her feet in the water and maybe collect a few shells. She started picking up some, trying not to notice that Aaron was watching her every move.

"Alex, come into the water with us!" called Pen some yards away.

Alex shook her head. "It's too cold for me!"

"It's not that bad!" said Logan before he dunked his uncle under the water.

Aaron soon burst to the surface, shaking himself and laughing. Alex found herself immobile as she watched him. With water dripping from his body, he was gorgeous. She curled her toes into the sand and suddenly wished he were tossing *her* into the water.

"Are you just going to stand there and stare?" said Aaron.

Alex scowled. "No. I'm looking for shells."

She studiously ignored him as she wandered along the shoreline. When an iridescent bit of shell caught her eye, she crouched and began digging. She was so aware of Aaron, though, that she didn't realize the bit of shell was actually a piece of glass until she felt the wicked sting of a cut across her palm.

She cried out as her palm began bleeding. It was pure agony when the saltwater spread across the wound. Tears pricked Alex's eyes, and she held up her hand, suddenly immobilized as she watched her palm bleed into the water.

Then a warm body was guiding her out of the water, and before she understood what was happening, Aaron was opening a bottle of water and pouring it onto her hand.

"It doesn't look too deep," he was saying, "but you should get checked out. Is your tetanus vaccine up to date?"

Alex blinked at him. "What?"

"Tetanus. What did you cut your hand on, anyway?"

"Um, I think it was glass. I'm not sure."

The burning pain was slowly dissipating as Aaron finished pouring the cold bottle of water.

"Do you have a small towel or something?" he asked.

"Here, use my bandana," said Gwen.

Alex hadn't realized that Gwen and Jocelyn had returned. Had they seen everything?

Aaron gazed up at her as he gently wrapped her hand in the purple bandana. "Is that better?" His voice was soft.

Alex felt like she couldn't breathe. It wasn't from the pain now: it was from the concern on Aaron's face. The way he touched her, like she was a delicate bit of porcelain.

Worst of all, he was so close that she could see the crystalline droplets of water hanging from his eyelashes. She could also see that his irises were ringed with gold. Had his eyes always looked like that? She felt like she would've noticed that before.

"Um, I'm okay," Alex stuttered. She pulled her hand away.

Aaron blinked. Then, the spell broken, he stepped away, and Alex felt like she could breathe again.

"Is she going to be okay?" asked Pen.

Aaron gave his niece a wan smile. "She'll be fine. Come on, let's get Logan."

Alex watched Aaron walk away, feeling frozen. She cradled her injured hand against her chest.

"Well," said Jocelyn from behind Alex. "That was interesting."

Alex couldn't look at her sister or Gwen. "I should get my hand looked at."

"Do you think you'll need stitches?" asked Gwen as they walked to their cars.

"I think it's already stopped bleeding." Alex inspected the cut; it was only oozing a little blood now. "The saltwater made it hurt like a bitch."

Jocelyn's eyes were narrowed at Alex, then her gaze would shift over Alex's shoulder.

"You can stay, if you want," said Alex lamely.

To Alex's surprise, Jocelyn patted her shoulder and then walked away without another word.

"Do I want to know what that's about?" said Alex.

Gwen shot her a strange look. "I guess we'll see," was her vague reply.

"Should we wait for her?"

Right then, Gwen received a text that made her laugh. "She says we don't have to wait for her."

"God, my sister is terrifying sometimes," muttered Alex.

WHEN AARON TURNED to see a blond woman marching toward him, he wondered if this was what some poor deer felt like when confronted with the barrel of a hunter's rifle.

"I need to talk to you," the woman—Jocelyn, he remembered—snapped at him. She even snapped her fingers.

Nonplussed, Aaron considered simply driving off without acknowledging her command. But Pen, who was about to get into the car, widened her eyes and said, "She looks mad."

Logan stuck his head out. "Who's mad? Is somebody fighting?"

"No one is fighting," replied Aaron firmly. To Pen, he said, "Get in the car. This will just be a second."

"You shouldn't leave kids unattended in a hot car." Logan grinned up at him like the cheeky monkey he was.

Aaron went around, turned on the car's AC, and gave them both stern looks that neither took seriously. Normally he would've told them to roll down their windows, but he had a feeling he didn't want them overhearing this conversation.

Jocelyn was tapping her foot, her arms crossed. She'd taken off her sunglasses, and Aaron was amused to see she already had a tan line on her face.

Although she looked nothing like her sister, Jocelyn and Alex shared the same stubborn jut of their chin, along with their fearsome gazes when crossed.

"What are you doing with my sister?" demanded Jocelyn without preamble.

Aaron let out a cross between a chuckle and a guffaw. "What am I doing? Besides binding a cut on her hand? Nothing."

"Look, I know my sister. I also know men. No man looks at a woman like you did back there if he doesn't care about her."

He decided staying calm was the best course of action. He didn't want to feed into Jocelyn's delusions, whatever they were.

"I was helping someone who needed it," he said slowly, like he was explaining something to a child. "I'm pretty sure if I'd ignored her, I'd be a pretty big asshole. Or a sociopath."

"I'm not just talking about her getting hurt." Jocelyn pointed a finger in Aaron's face, a finger he had the sudden desire to slap away. "I'm talking about how you kept ogling her. While your kids were watching, I should add."

Aaron scowled and pushed her hand aside. "Look, I don't know what your problem is, but you're making a mountain out of a molehill. I'm not interested in your sister. If this is some weird way of getting me to go out with her—"

Jocelyn laughed coldly. "God, you're arrogant. You date one woman while you can't keep your eyes off another. I'm pretty sure there are a few choice words for men like that."

"Felicity and I are just dating." Realizing he sounded defensive, he softened his tone. "You're seeing something that's not there."

For a moment, Jocelyn looked unsure. But that stubbornness that seemed to be genetic in the Gray family took over.

"Maybe I'm wrong," she said, "but I just want to tell you that if you hurt my sister, I will make it my mission to make your life hell. I know everybody on this island. You won't be able even to get a package of toilet paper without hassle."

"I'll just get it delivered, then."

"I'm serious."

"So am I."

They stared each other down, both waiting for the other to capitulate.

"There's nothing between me and your sister. And there never will be," said Aaron quietly but firmly.

As he drove home, Pen and Logan pestering him about his conversation with Jocelyn, Aaron felt like the earth under his feet was shifting with every step.

Most of all, he knew he had to avoid being around Alex. She was bad for him, for one. But she also wasn't the right person to be a mother for Logan and Pen. She was too impulsive, too emotional. He needed someone who was calm. Steady.

Boring, his mind whispered.

He pushed the thought aside. Felicity wasn't boring.

She just wasn't Alex.

CHAPTER THIRTEEN

Aaron kept his promise to himself. He threw himself into courting and wooing Felicity, taking her out as much as their schedules allowed. By the end of the month, he finally had time to invite her over for dinner.

Time, but also the assurance that Logan wouldn't act up while Felicity was over. Although Aaron had naively assumed that with enough rational conversation he could get the kids to agree with him, he'd realized that in some instances, the only sure way to gain compliance was through bribery.

And so Logan got a new video game, while Pen got a few new books, in Aaron's attempt to keep them from saying or doing anything that would scare Felicity away.

"Don't ask her if we're getting married, or if we've kissed—"

That statement was met with simultaneous looks and groans of disgust from Logan and Pen.

By the end of Aaron's list of demands, Pen had said, "So you just want us to say nothing?"

Aaron had decided, rather unwisely he'd realized too late, to make the dinner himself. How hard could it be to make a nice meal? Too hard, he'd realized after the chicken he'd put in the oven had become dry, inedible rocks.

He'd ended up ordering pizza, which arrived only a few minutes after Felicity's arrival.

"Aaron tried to cook," said Logan with a smirk, "but he burned it all."

Aaron shot him a look. "I changed my mind. That's all."

Felicity smiled in her quiet way. "Who doesn't like pizza?"

Dinner with Pen and Logan went as well as Aaron expected. Despite Logan rudely asking about Felicity's face —which she answered calmly—and Pen squirting ranch dressing all over the table accidentally, the dinner was a success.

Except the fact that Aaron couldn't stop thinking about another woman. As Felicity talked about her favorite books with Pen, Aaron couldn't help but wonder what books would be on Alex's list. When Felicity talked about how she liked to go birdwatching, he couldn't help but imagine Alex being incapable of sitting still to watch birds.

Near the end of the evening, Pen and Logan blessedly upstairs, Aaron brought Felicity a glass of wine. After clinking glasses and taking a sip, he leaned over and pressed his lips to hers.

But he felt nothing. No fireworks, no chemistry. What was his problem? She smelled good; she looked pretty in her green sweater dress. She was smart; she was kind. She'd been great with the kids.

His stomach plummeted. He felt like someone had just pushed him off a cliff into the unknown.

Apparently, Alexandra Gray had infected him, and he didn't know if he could—or wanted to—find the cure. Worst of all, he hated to admit that Jocelyn had been right. *Damn her.*

He drew away from Felicity, scrubbing his face. "I don't think this is working," he said.

Felicity blinked. "What?"

Aaron instantly wanted to slap himself. *Way to break it to her easy*, he thought scathingly.

"Look, you're an awesome, nice woman," he began, but Felicity held up a hand.

"If you say the words, 'it's not you, it's me,' I might scream," she said.

Aaron grimaced. "Would it matter if that statement were true?" He took her hand, but she pulled it back after a brief moment. "You have to feel it, too. I mean, the lack of chemistry."

She tucked a strand of hair behind her ear. "You are straightforward, aren't you?"

"Shit. I'm sorry. I'm fucking this up completely. I'm an idiot."

"I do like you," she murmured, and Aaron wanted to bolt right out the front door. "I thought there was something between us. But if you don't feel it, then, well..." She gripped the fabric of her dress. "I should go."

Aaron couldn't help but notice the tears in her eyes. What a selfish son of a bitch he was, he thought bitterly.

"I'm sorry," he said. He gave her a hug, which she didn't return.

"I'd ask you why, but I don't think I want to know the reason." Felicity smiled sadly. "Ignorance is bliss, I guess."

Although he offered to walk her to her car, she declined. He watched her drive away, his anger at himself building with every passing minute.

Most of all, he was angry at the woman who'd taken hold of him, the woman who'd been haunting him since that night on the beach.

Grabbing his car keys, he drove to the bookstore, only realizing too late that the bookstore was already closed. Getting out of his car, he peered through the window. He could make out a light coming from Alex's office.

He knocked on the window. When that failed, he called Alex and said tersely, "I'm outside."

Alex eventually came out, her expression confused. She unlocked the entrance but didn't open the door further to let him inside.

"What is it? You look like you've seen a ghost," she said. Her face paled. "Is something wrong with the kids?"

Aaron glanced away. "How's your hand?"

"My hand? You came all the way here to ask me that?" Alex showed him her palm. "All healed. You didn't answer my question, by the way."

"The kids are fine. They're at home enjoying all their new things."

Aaron was breathing hard. Worst of all, his entire body felt like it was on fire just from being close to Alex. He wasn't even kissing her. Why did she have this power over him?

"I ended things with Felicity," he ground out.

"Oh."

"That's all you have to say? 'Oh'? Don't you care that your friend is at home, crying?"

Alex bristled. "What is wrong with you? Of course I care! But I'm not the one who made her cry."

"You're just as guilty as me." Aaron knew he was being an asshole. But he pushed Alex aside, crowding her, until he'd pushed her against a wall. Her breasts rose and fell with every panting breath.

"You set us up. You pushed us together, even after I kissed you—twice. I think most people would say that either makes you a masochist, or maybe a sadist," he said.

"Fuck you, Aaron Morrison. I don't know what game you're playing, but you can get the hell out of my store—"

Aaron didn't want to talk anymore. Swooping down, he caught her mouth in a bruising kiss.

ALEX LET herself fall into the kiss, but only for a moment. Even as her body was screaming at her to continue, her mind knew she couldn't.

Pushing Aaron away, she wiped her mouth and stalked away.

"You don't have anything to say?" He followed her, relentless. "Hey! Don't walk away from me!"

Alex whirled on him. "This is my store. Get out or I'll call the cops."

"Baby, I *own* this entire building. The cops won't do a damned thing."

She snarled at him. He was laughing down at her, and she wanted to claw his eyes out. Instead, she picked up the nearest book and chucked it straight at his head.

He ducked just in time. "Alex, what the fuck—?"

She threw another book. It sideswiped his shoulder.

"You—" Another book thrown. "Can—" Another. "Go—" One last one. "To hell!"

Aaron didn't dodge the last book. He let it hit him in the chest, but based on his expression, he'd barely felt the blow.

Alex was panting now. To her frustration, Aaron didn't seem remotely fazed by her book throwing.

"Are you done?" he asked.

"Not sure yet. How about we go to the nonfiction section, and we try a few big ones?"

Before she could make good on her threat, Aaron seized her by the waist, holding her captive in his strong embrace.

"I never wanted this," he said, sounding like he was in agony. "That night on the beach—I've never stopped thinking about it. And I've fucking *tried.* I've tried my hardest to get you out of my head, but it's like you're an incurable disease."

Alex glared at him. "Wow, thanks for the compliment."

"It wasn't a compliment." He gripped her harder. "Nothing about you is good. You drive me insane. You're obnoxious, stubborn, nosey, entitled—"

"And you're a greedy, heartless son of a bitch who doesn't care that he's ruining people's lives! Don't act like you're a saint, either."

Despite his harsh words, his hands roved over her back down to her ass. He pressed her closer until she could feel the outline of his hardened cock against her hip.

"I want you more than I've ever wanted any woman." His voice was a rasp in her ear. "I want to fuck you until this thing between us goes away."

Alex swallowed. She hated that she was trembling. Most of all, she hated how she wanted him to keep touching her. Or that she reveled in how good he smelled, or how strong his arms were around her.

"Why am I such a bad choice for you?" she whispered. Her chest felt unbearably tight.

"Because you aren't right for me. We both know it. We'd kill each other in the end."

"You don't know that." But even as she said the words, she wasn't sure if she believed them.

Aaron began kissing her throat, his breath hot, his tongue tracing patterns that made her melt.

"It's just lust. It'll pass." He sucked on the lobe of her ear.

As Aaron continued to kiss her, Alex couldn't help but touch him back. She pushed his shirt up, wanting to feel the heat of his skin.

"That's right. Touch me. Don't fucking stop," he muttered.

Alex was caught in a maelstrom, and she didn't know if she wanted to be rescued.

Then he was kissing her again, and she was letting him take her further into the darkness of the store. They tumbled onto a small couch in the back, Aaron maneuvering them both so Alex was lying on top of him. He'd already rucked her shirt up to her breasts and was unfastening her bra with nimble fingers.

Alex groaned when he palmed her breast with one

hand, the other raking through her hair. "What are we doing?" she breathed.

Aaron shook his head. "No talking. Don't think. Just feel."

Alex didn't need to be told twice, especially when he sat up and took her breast in his mouth. Alex rolled her hips, needing more friction against her aching core.

But as she bounced and moved against him, she blurted in between kisses, "I don't have a condom on me."

Aaron paused. It seemed to take him a moment for his brain to understand what she'd just said. Then he shrugged. "Me, either. It's fine."

"I'm not having sex without one. I'm not on birth control."

His lips twitched. "And the last thing I need is another kid." He kissed her lightly. "We won't go all the way."

Alex instantly felt calmer, and as the kissing and touching reached a fever pitch, she nearly wondered why she'd made that stipulation. She was desperate for him, to the point that he chuckled at her.

"You want me to make you feel good," he whispered in her ear as he pushed her jeans and panties down. He cupped her sex, groaning when he found her wet already. "I don't think it'll take long."

"Weren't you the one who told me to stop talking?" Alex admonished.

Aaron thrust a finger inside her at the same time he rubbed her clit. Alex's eyes nearly rolled into the back of her head.

He played with her, drawing out her orgasm, making

her moan and beg. If she'd had any pride left, she would've been embarrassed by how desperate she sounded.

Aaron pushed another finger inside her. "Oh, you're close."

Alex bit his shoulder. She rolled her hips in an effort to get him to go faster. "Please—" she moaned.

Aaron kissed her as his fingers moved faster, his thumb circling her clit with more pressure. Alex began shivering as her orgasm built. When she came with a scream, Aaron caught the sound in his mouth.

In her haze, Alex felt Aaron move her hand to his cock. She traced its outline, but even as she did so, she felt a cold anxiety growing inside her chest.

When Aaron began to unbutton his jeans, Alex jerked her hand away and scrambled to the opposite side of the couch.

"Alex, what is it?"

Aaron tried to touch her, but she jumped up and put her hands up.

"Um, sorry. I just—it was a little too much." She nearly fell on her face since her pants were around her ankles. When Aaron rose to help her, she had to restrain herself from smacking his hands away. But he simply helped her get dressed, saying nothing.

"Did I go too fast?" He touched her cheek. "I didn't mean to scare you."

Alex felt like she was hearing Aaron's words from underwater. Memories of Devon filled her, memories of him wanting her to do things she didn't want to do, but what choice did she have—?

She was nearly hyperventilating right then. In a squeaky voice, she said, "Please go. Please. I need to be alone."

"Alex—"

"Go! Get out of here!" She nearly screamed the words.

Aaron's face shuttered. Then he left without saying another word.

CHAPTER FOURTEEN

Devon had been good to Alex, at least at first. On the first date, he'd paid for everything, although Alex hadn't known how he'd been able to afford it.

He didn't have a job, at least as far as Alex knew. Yet he would bring her flowers, or chocolates, or balloons, often-times in the middle of a school day.

It was only later that Alex realized he'd almost always given her those gifts with an audience present.

At fifteen, Alex had only kissed a few boys. She knew about sex from reading romance novels, but she didn't know that some boys could turn your head to the point that you'd do whatever they asked.

Devon was good at that. When Alex was over at his house one night, he squeezed her breast out of the blue. They hadn't even kissed with tongue yet. Then, before Alex could react, he reached inside her shirt and flicked her nipple.

"You like that?" His smile was predatory. "Your face is red. You like it, you little slut."

Devon would soon push her boundaries, seeing if she'd tell him no. When Alex told him she wanted to go home after he'd pushed too far, he pouted and complained.

"I just got you that bracelet. You're so ungrateful," he told her, looking truly hurt. "I thought you loved me."

Even as a small part of her hated their relationship, Alex also found herself obsessed with Devon's every move. When he flirted with other girls, she'd explode. When he'd give her the silent treatment for some imagined offense, she'd twist herself in knots to get his forgiveness.

The first time they had sex, Alex went home the next day feeling nothing. She wondered why. Shouldn't she be elated? But it was like all emotions had disappeared.

When Jocelyn finally got her way, separating the young couple and getting Devon into trouble, Alex felt like her heart would never recover from losing Devon. Although the charges against him were eventually dropped, it was enough that he never contacted Alex again. Soon after, he moved away from the island for good.

Sitting in the dark of the bookstore, Alex remembered. It had only been with time and maturity that she'd realized how Devon had abused her, manipulating her into doing things she hadn't truly wanted. He'd been toxic.

Yet she'd loved him with her entire being. Even now, she didn't fully understand how she could have loved and hated the same person, and at one point, at the same time.

Alex scrubbed at her face. She was surprised to find tears. It wasn't as if she hadn't had sex with guys other than Devon, and she'd never reacted like this before. But there was something about Aaron that twisted her up in knots.

She sat in the dark for a while, crying silently, wondering

what the hell she was doing. She'd just fooled around with the same guy who was dating her best friend. Well, had been dating.

Alex hated herself in that moment. Everything her sister had always said about her was true: she was impulsive. Selfish. *Stupid*, she thought bitterly.

Only a stupid woman would get involved with a guy who could never be hers.

When Alex heard the door to the bookstore open, she froze. She hadn't even thought about locking it after Aaron had pushed his way inside. Her heart pounding, she waited for Aaron to reappear from the shadows.

But it wasn't Aaron: it was Gwen. Her hair in a messy topknot, wearing pajamas, it looked like Gwen had come from bed.

Gwen frowned over at Alex. "Are you sitting here in the dark, alone?"

Alex just started crying all over again.

After some persuasion and assurances that she didn't mind in the least, Gwen took Alex to her house.

"Is Jack…?" Alex asked before she stepped inside the cozy bungalow.

"I told him to stay in the bedroom. He has to be up super early, anyway."

It wasn't that Alex didn't like Gwen's fiancé. She just didn't want a bigger audience for her meltdown.

Gwen handed Alex a hot mug of tea as they both settled on the overstuffed living room couch. Alex sniffled, her head starting to pound.

"How did you know I was in the bookstore?" Alex asked suddenly.

"Aaron told me."

Alex nearly spilled her hot tea all over herself. "Aaron? What, he came here?"

"We exchanged numbers a few weeks ago when talking business. He texted me."

Alex stared down at the contents of her mug, completely stunned. "What did he say?"

"Just that you were at the store and needed help. Honestly, it was so random that it scared me. But he just said that you were upset and needed a friend."

Alex felt tears threatening again. Feeling silly, she tried to hide them, but it was no use. Apparently she was just going to spend the whole night crying.

Gwen reached out and patted her hand. "Tell me what happened. All of it."

Alex slowly told Gwen the story about her and Aaron from beginning to end, feeling a hot flush creep into her face with every word. Gwen, bless her, didn't say a word, and her expression stayed neutral throughout.

As far as the Devon story, Alex was tempted to skip over it. But then she remembered how Gwen had struggled with her own issues after her first marriage had ended. Her ex-husband had told her she was frigid in bed, and Gwen had taken that cruelty to heart.

By the end of her recital, Alex felt exhausted, but even worse, she felt ashamed. Deeply, deeply ashamed.

"You've gotten yourself into quite a pickle," said Gwen finally.

"You're judging me. I can hear it in your voice."

"No, I'm not. I'm not Jocelyn."

Alex's eyes widened. Gwen was the last person to say a harsh word about anybody.

Gwen looked abashed. "Sorry. Don't tell her I said that. But I'm not here to make you feel badly. God knows I've made my own stupid mistakes, too. Nobody's perfect."

"But what about Felicity?" whispered Alex.

"Aaron ended things, right? Now, maybe he should've waited, I don't know, at least twenty-four hours before moving on to you, but…" Gwen sighed. "Isn't that between him and Felicity?"

"I pushed them together. I wanted it to work out."

"That's what I don't get. You both are into each other. So why is Felicity even in the equation?"

Alex remembered Aaron's angry words, how he'd told her point-blank that she wasn't the right woman for him. How she was more like the literal plague to him than a person he'd care about.

"We're bad for each other. We just fight," said Alex.

"Sounds like you're both fighting against your feelings and taking it out on each other."

"What an astute observation." Alex's tone was wry.

"Hey, am I wrong? You both like to have your way. You're both stubborn, opinionated." Gwen shrugged. "It makes sense that you'd butt heads. But that doesn't mean it'd always be like that."

"I wish I had your optimism. My track record with guys…" Alex's mouth twisted. "It's not great."

"Neither is mine, babe. My first husband was a real loser. Then I found Jack. It took a second, though. I was too blind and stubborn to believe we could be together. But he proved me wrong."

Alex sipped her tea, silently contemplating. The difference between Jack and Aaron was that Jack had wanted Gwen from the beginning.

Aaron? He wanted Alex and resented her for it. It wasn't exactly a great way to start off a relationship.

"When I was with Devon," said Alex softly, setting her empty mug on the coffee table, "I thought for sure he was my soulmate. But he was hurting me, and I didn't even know it. It was right in front of my face. So how can I believe something with Aaron would be different?"

Gwen gave her a sad look. "Aaron seems like a decent guy. Or are you saying that he forced you…?" Her forehead crinkled with concern.

Alex shook her head. "I wanted him. I still want him."

"Then start there. See where it goes."

"You're assuming Aaron wants to see where it goes. He's already told me I'm not right for him." Alex scowled. "Which I'm pretty sure means he doesn't think I'm good enough for him."

"If that's the case, then screw him. He's missing out. You're amazing, Alex. Yes, you have your moments, but you've grown up a lot in the past few years. I've seen it myself. I'm proud to call you my friend."

Alex's eyes watered. "Oh God, stop. I'm going to start crying for the thousandth time!"

"Love you, too." Gwen hugged her. "And I know you'll figure this out."

Alex didn't have the heart to tell her friend that she didn't feel nearly as confident.

When Alex arrived home, she was relieved to find Felicity already in bed. She didn't know if she should be honest with Felicity or not. But what would the point be? If she and Aaron were never going to be official, telling Felicity the dirty details would only hurt her.

It was nearing midnight, but Alex wasn't sleepy. She grabbed some chips from the pantry and turned the TV on. She tried to watch a few trashy reality shows, but none of them could hold her attention.

She could only think about Aaron.

She'd assumed he'd left the store angry. Maybe he had, but he'd still texted Gwen. He'd been worried about Alex enough to reach out to a woman he didn't know well.

He could've just gone home without another word. Alex wouldn't have blamed him.

Despite her best efforts, she couldn't help the warm and fuzzy feeling spreading through her limbs. As she finally began to fall asleep, she wondered if maybe, just maybe, Gwen's optimism was warranted.

CHAPTER FIFTEEN

Aaron realized that he'd made a huge mistake in moving to a tiny island. It meant that no matter how hard he tried, he'd run into the people he most wanted to avoid seeing.

Back in Seattle, he'd gotten tired of feeling invisible, moving through a sea of people but never feeling seen. Now, he desperately wished to return to that kind of invisibility.

After the ordeal at Alex's store, Aaron threw himself into his work. He also avoided the coffee shop across the street from Alex's store, He only went to the grocery store early in the morning, when he knew she would either be at work or asleep. He avoided Lyn's, and the bed-and-breakfast, and if he could've locked himself in his house, he would have.

But the kids needed rides, and Aaron needed food, so becoming a true recluse was out of reach at the moment.

On Halloween, both Pen and Logan were dressing up to go trick-or-treating with their friends. When Aaron had pointed out that they were both too old for trick-or-treating, they'd given him looks that told him how wrong he was.

"I've seen high schoolers going around on Halloween," said Pen, adjusting her fairy wings and checking her glittery makeup in the hall mirror.

"Pretty sure anyone who tried that when I was in high school would be told to get lost," replied Aaron.

"You're old. Things are different now." Pen shrugged a single shoulder and headed out.

As far as Logan, he'd been behaving himself lately, so Aaron figured allowing him a chance to prove he could make good choices was a good idea. Aaron just hoped his tentative trust in his nephew wasn't misplaced.

"No pranks, no harassing people, no peeing in bushes —" Aaron was saying.

Logan rolled his eyes. He was going as Spiderman, but Aaron could still see the kid's eyes through the mask. "I'm not gonna do anything," whined Logan.

"Pretty sure I've heard those exact words before."

"I'm not. I promise. Can I go now? Eric is waiting for me."

Aaron let him go, assured that the neighborhood would also be watching out for Logan and the other kids.

Returning to his office, Aaron tried to get work done, but he couldn't concentrate. It didn't help that his doorbell kept ringing with trick-or-treaters all evening.

His brain was coming up with all kinds of scenarios where Logan could get into trouble. Worst of all, Aaron remembered how he and Jason had egged a house one Halloween and had been brought home by the cops. Their parents had been livid.

Did kids still egg houses? Aaron didn't know. He felt like he was a thousand years old.

When he ran out of candy, he turned off the porch lights and headed out. He had no destination in mind. Mostly, he just didn't want to sit at home with his thoughts.

Kids and parents were still out, filling the sidewalks, the bright colors of the kids' costumes making Aaron smile. He saw the standard ghosts and witches, along with lots of superheroes, princesses, and a few strange ones, like a roll of sushi or a fire hydrant.

Two little girls were running up the sidewalk toward him, both of them dressed in bright pink tutus and tiaras. They nearly collided straight into Aaron's legs.

"Lola! Greta!" a woman called. She hurried after them, her expression harried. "I'm so sorry. They lose their minds around candy. Lola! Do not rip that spider off the railing! This is not our house!"

Aaron turned to see the girl in question attempting to take down a spider decoration that was bigger than her head.

"I told Elliot we should put them on leashes, but no, he thinks that's inhumane." The woman rolled her eyes, then her gaze caught on Aaron. "I don't know you. Are you new here?"

"Um, yes?" He was wondering the same thing.

"I'm Bekah. You might know my sister-in-law, Gwen. I grew up on the island, although now my family and I live in Seattle."

Aaron introduced himself, but Bekah was soon chasing after the girls again. Apparently Greta had decided that she was going to try to put as many candies in her mouth as she could manage.

Aaron watched the scene, bemused, when he heard a voice that made him freeze. The trio—Gwen, Felicity, and Alex—came up the sidewalk. Only Alex was dressed up, wearing some kind of witch costume with a gigantic purple hat.

Aaron's eyes met Alex's. Alex stopped in her tracks, which made Felicity run into her.

"What is—? Oh." Felicity caught Aaron's gaze and looked away just as quickly. Then she hurried off in the direction Bekah and the girls went.

"Well, this is awkward," blurted Alex.

Gwen covered her mouth to smother a laugh. Aaron just shot Alex an annoyed look.

"I think Bekah needs me. Um, have fun, you two," said Gwen.

Aaron nearly begged Gwen to stay, but Gwen was faster than he would've expected.

"Um," said Alex. "What's up?"

"Seriously? You're asking me *that*?"

"Well, you weren't going to say anything. Or do you just want to stand here and glare at me?"

Aaron was considering it. It didn't help that Alex's costume was slinky and revealing. It showed off her curves, while her witch's hat made her look especially devious. Or maybe it was the look in her eyes. Either way, Aaron had to resist the urge in dragging her off into the bushes to have his wicked way with her.

"Thanks, you know." Alex was twisting her hands now. "For texting Gwen the other night."

"I told her not to tell you." He frowned.

"Commanding people to do whatever you want isn't the best strategy." Alex's expression turned serious once again. "What happened at the end... it wasn't your fault. I just freaked out."

Considering Aaron had been twisting himself in knots trying to understand what had happened that night, he was skeptical. "I pushed you too far. I'm sorry," he said quietly.

"I'm sorry, too. I never wanted to hurt anyone."

Aaron barely stifled a chuckle. "I'm pretty sure you wanted to strangle me on more than one occasion."

"Only when you deserved it."

They gazed at each other, the moment stretching until it felt like they were the only two people in the world. Aaron reached out and brushed a finger along her jaw.

Then he put more space between them. "We're not good for each other, clearly. I'll leave you alone."

Alex's eyes widened. "Is that what you want?"

No. "Yes."

"Okay. Maybe you're right. If not for us, then for Felicity."

Guilt hit Aaron like an arrow to the gut. "How is she?"

"She won't talk to me."

"Does she know about...?"

Alex shook her head, her eyes wide. "No way. And I'm not going to tell her. Are you?"

"Fuck no. That'd be cruel."

"Okay. Good."

Aaron looked off into the distance, wondering where the group had gone. "What about Gwen? She doesn't seem great at keeping her mouth shut."

"She won't say anything because she knows it'll just hurt Felicity."

"Then that's that."

Alex tucked a piece of hair behind her ear. Then she moved in to hug him. The hug was so brief that Aaron didn't have time to react before Alex walked away into the darkness.

ALEX WATCHED Felicity from the corner of her eye. After their run-in with Aaron, Felicity had barely spoken the rest of the evening.

Taking off her witch's hat, Alex felt like she should say *something*, but she was tongue-tied. She couldn't remember the last time she didn't have anything to say.

"Was Aaron ever interested in me?" said Felicity, jolting Alex out of her thoughts.

Felicity's voice was even, calm, but Alex knew her friend well enough to hear the steel underneath the calm.

"Isn't that something you should ask him?" Alex replied.

"I saw you two. He couldn't stop looking at you. I didn't even exist. So I think you can tell me the answer to my question."

Alex's mouth went dry. "I don't know what you're talking about."

"Oh, come on, Alex. Don't do this. I'm not stupid, despite what you all seem to think."

"I've never thought you were stupid."

"Naive, then? Oh, poor little Felicity. Poor, sad, virginal Felicity." Felicity's face darkened. "No man would want her unless you twisted their arm. Is that what you were all thinking? Laughing about it behind my back?"

Alex stared, stunned. "What? No—"

"Then tell me the truth for once. Tell me that your whole 'I want to help you and Aaron' thing was because you wanted to help. Tell me the truth, Alex."

"Aaron liked you. Why else would he go out with you?"

"You assured me that whatever had happened between you two was over. You promised me, and I believed you. But now I'm wondering if you were lying. What was in it for you?"

"And why are you always the victim? You never had to date him. Nobody made you."

Felicity laughed, but it was a bitter sound. "The fact that you won't answer my question tells me pretty much everything I need to know. Why do I get the feeling that this was about the bookstore?"

Tears were shining in her eyes now. "I thought you were my friend, but I guess not. I guess what you want is more important. If other people get hurt, well, who cares, right? Who cares if the ugly chick gets screwed in the end?"

"I've *never* thought of you like that. Nobody does. Surely you know that," said Alex, pleading now.

Felicity rubbed her forehead, pushing her hair away from her face, showing the large birthmark that she took such pains to hide. "You don't know what you're talking about. Don't tell me how I should feel."

"I'm not, I'm just saying that no one thinks you're pathetic or ugly or whatever else you've convinced yourself. Aaron was interested in you. He told me so himself."

Felicity's lips twisted. "Not for myself, but to be a mom

for his kids. Did he mention that? He wasn't *attracted* to me. No, that'd be too much to ask."

Alex felt like she was sinking deeper and deeper into quicksand. "I'm sorry," she whispered finally.

"If you want to be with Aaron, fine. You have my blessing. He never wanted me to begin with. I just wish you could've been honest, you know? You should've just told me." Felicity's voice broke.

"Liss—"

"I'm serious. I'm not going to stand between you two. I saw the way you guys were looking at each other."

Now Alex was crying. "I don't even know what I want anymore. I'm so confused."

"That's not my problem."

Alex flinched, but she couldn't disagree.

Felicity continued. "I'm still angry with you. I still think you're keeping something from me. But I'm not going to tell you to not see him." Her smile was bitter. "Aren't I a good friend?"

"You are. Better than I've been."

"I'm going to bed. And then I'm going to go stay with Gwen, probably, to get some space."

"You don't have to go. I should be the one to go."

"It hurts too much right now to be in this apartment."

When Alex tried to give Felicity a hug, Felicity gently pushed her hands away and went to her room without another word.

CHAPTER SIXTEEN

Alex threw herself into work in order to avoid thinking about her personal life. Felicity had been staying with Gwen for two weeks now, and Alex didn't know if she'd ever return. Of course, Felicity was too responsible to stop paying rent. When Alex came home to find an envelope with a check under the door from Felicity, she had the urge to go straight to Gwen's and get this situation resolved.

As the holidays approached, the bookstore usually saw a nice uptick in sales. Even better, Lila White's signing was scheduled for the beginning of December. Alex had finally confirmed a date and was now furiously pushing the news in the local press. With every ticket and every preordered book purchased for the signing, Alex felt dangerous hope blossoming inside her.

"Do you think the bookstore can have that many people inside it at one time?" Chris asked as he and Alex looked over the ticket sales.

"We might need to have people wait outside."

"In December? In the rain? Is there money in the budget for a canopy?"

"We'll be lucky if we can afford a few extra umbrellas," muttered Alex.

Although the ticket sales were going well, Alex wasn't sure this signing would be enough to save the bookstore. It hadn't helped that Aaron had essentially gone MIA. They hadn't spoken since they'd run into each other on Halloween. As far as Alex knew, the rent increase would go into effect by February first regardless.

"We just need to market the hell out of this signing," she kept saying to herself. "If we can get enough buzz, enough books ordered, and then get people signed up for our mailing list to keep them coming back."

She was full of ideas, to the point that she wished she weren't living alone just so she could talk them over with somebody. Felicity had always been a good sounding board.

Alex had texted Felicity twice. Both texts had received short replies without any follow-up texts. Alex could tell by their tone that Felicity still wasn't in the mood to have a heart-to-heart.

Worst of all, Alex couldn't stop thinking about Aaron. She constantly dreamed about him, felt his hands on her body, and she'd awaken with her heart pounding and her core aching. More than once, she'd nearly called him and told him to come over just to assuage the ache only he could fill.

It didn't help that Pen still came by the bookstore nearly once a week. Alex always had to restrain herself from asking if Uncle Aaron had come with her.

On Thanksgiving, Alex spent the day with Jocelyn, their

dad, Pete, and Luke. Jocelyn cooked the entire meal that everyone raved about. Jocelyn brushed off the compliments, even though Alex knew her sister loved the praise. Based on how much they'd all eaten, she totally deserved it.

"I'm surprised Felicity and Gwen didn't join us," said Luke after they'd eaten. "Joss, didn't you invite them?"

Jocelyn shrugged. "Gwen said she and Jack wanted to do their own thing." Her gaze moved toward Alex. "And apparently with Felicity, as well."

Alex sipped her wine and avoided her sister's prying eyes.

"Why do I get the feeling there's something I don't know about?" asked Pete.

At his feet was Jocelyn's pet rabbit, Fluffernutter, who was enjoying a Thanksgiving snack of romaine lettuce and a few bites of apple. Alex petted the rabbit's silky ears, which made Fluffer close his eyes in ecstasy.

"Felicity moved out," replied Alex tersely. "Or she's not living with me right now."

Pete frowned. "Did you two get into a fight?"

"Yeah, did you two fight?" This from Jocelyn.

Alex hadn't wanted to give all of the dirty details about Aaron, Felicity, and herself to her family. And the last thing she wanted was her sister to judge her.

But Jocelyn said nothing. She seemed contemplative. It was strange, and it made Alex want to head home and lock her door. A contemplative Jocelyn tended to mean she was putting together some nefarious plan.

"Felicity just needed some space. She's still paying rent," said Alex.

"Really? That's nice of her," said Luke.

When Luke and Jocelyn went to the kitchen to begin plating dessert, Pete came over and put a hand on Alex's shoulder. "You don't seem yourself," he said quietly, squeezing gently. "Anything you want to tell your dad?"

Alex picked up Fluffer and placed him in her lap. He tolerated her petting him for a few moments before he wanted to get down again.

"The rabbit wants to eat his apple," said Pete with a chuckle. He handed Fluffer the last bite that had rolled near Pete's foot. "This guy will bite off your finger for a piece of apple if you're not careful."

"I know. He did the same to me when I was rabbit-sitting," said Alex. Sighing, she then added, "Everything's just a mess right now. But I'll figure it out."

"Joss mentioned that there was a guy." Pete raised an eyebrow. "Is there a guy I need to threaten?"

"No threats needed. We aren't good for each other. So it's over before it even began."

"Hmmm. You don't sound convinced."

Alex shrugged. "I'll get over him eventually."

"You know, sweetheart, I never thought any guy would be good enough for you, or your sister. When Jocelyn married Luke out of the blue, I could've taken him out back and broken his kneecaps. But then I saw how much they cared for each other and how much he loves your sister."

Pete cleared his throat. "Point being, I want the same for you. If you think this guy could be the one, don't let him go. I know you'll regret it."

Alex swallowed against the lump in her throat. "It's not that simple."

"Is he married?" Now Pete was scowling.

"No! No, he's not married. But he was dating Felicity, but that's over and…" Alex sighed. "I told you it was complicated."

"Ah. I think I understand now. Well, I know you'll do the right thing, which also means having to be brave, too. Sometimes the scariest things in life are also the things you want more than anything."

THANKSGIVING at the Morrison house was a monumental failure. First, Aaron overcooked the turkey to the point it was nearly inedible. He also put too much salt in the gravy, and the mashed potatoes were lumpy yet gluey at the same time.

The food notwithstanding, though, the kids were in a mood. Pen had woken up and had been emotional all day, while Logan had sulked in his room until Aaron had to nearly threaten him to come downstairs for dinner. Then they both complained about the food, and it took all of Aaron's self-control not to explode.

It didn't help that this time of year always reminded him —and the kids, too—of their parents. Aaron had always done Thanksgiving with Jason, and then when Jason had gotten married and started a family, they'd been added to the celebration.

Their mom would sometimes join them. After their father had died, their mom had moved to the other side of the country and hadn't had much contact with either of her sons.

So Jason and Aaron created their own family celebrations. Jason would make the turkey, and most of the sides, because Aaron couldn't be trusted in the kitchen. But Aaron would help with all the other tasks: dishwashing, cleaning, setting the table. He hadn't minded.

But this year was the first year without Jason and Ashley, and Aaron had woken up with his heart hurting. He'd wanted to chuck the turkey out the window when he couldn't cook it just like Jason used to.

"Can I go to my room?" Logan kept asking after he'd barely touched his food. "I want to play my new game."

"It's Thanksgiving. You can live without video games for one evening," snapped Aaron.

Logan crossed his arms and sank into his chair, his scowl never leaving his face.

Pen, for her part, had been crying at the drop of a hat all day. When Aaron had told her to set the table, she'd started crying, saying that her mom had always done that task.

"Pen, there's no reason to cry," Aaron had said, at a loss.

"You don't get it! You never get it!"

And so now the dinner was the three of them, sitting in silence, barely eating, their memories swarming them like locusts. In that moment, Aaron had the horrible thought that he wished he'd never taken in his brother's kids.

Guilt made his stomach sink. He knew he was just sad and frustrated, but the combination of regret and guilt was nearly too much to bear.

Most of all, he just wished his brother were here now. Jason would know what to do.

"I want to go upstairs," whined Logan in a voice that Aaron couldn't stand. "Why can't I?"

"I'm not hungry," Pen said in a similarly whiney voice.

Aaron's temples were pounding. "Fine. Go. Dinner is over."

Logan jumped from his chair and ran upstairs before Aaron could tell him to take his plate into the kitchen. He considered telling him to return, but he didn't have the energy.

"You go, too," he said to Pen softly. "I'll take care of the dishes."

Aaron felt like he was going to burst out of his skin. He had to get out of the house. He didn't care that it was pouring down rain, or that it was Thanksgiving. He just had the sudden, intense urge to see Alex. To hold her, kiss her, to make her know that he couldn't keep avoiding her like this.

After letting the kids know he was going out for an hour or two, Aaron drove straight to Alex's. But he stayed in his car, watching her window, wondering if he was completely insane.

He also realized that he had no idea if she were even home. It was a holiday, after all. Normal people would be with their families.

When he saw her curtains move, though, he knew she was home. He got out of his car, not caring that the rain was immediately soaking his shirt and hair. He hadn't even grabbed a jacket in his desperation to get the hell out of Dodge.

Alex opened her door and looked like she didn't recognize him. "Aaron? What are you doing here?"

He answered her by taking her into his arms and kissing her.

CHAPTER SEVENTEEN

Alex didn't have time to wonder why Aaron was at her apartment, dripping from the rain. His mouth roved over her own, hot and desperate. His hands were seemingly everywhere at once: cupping her breasts, squeezing her ass, sifting through her hair.

She finally forced herself to say, nearly gasping, "What...?"

"Do you want me?" His expression was inscrutable.

Annoyed now, she snapped, "What do you think?"

He grinned and swept her into his arms, kicking her door closed.

"Are you alone?" he asked suddenly. "I should've made sure—"

"I'm alone," replied Alex firmly. Then, because she didn't want to think about consequences or if this was a good idea, she brought his face down for another searing kiss.

He found her bedroom, setting her on her feet, never

breaking the kiss as they stripped out of their clothes. Aaron laughed when he struggled to take off his wet jeans.

"I guess the cold hasn't affected you too much," said Alex as she cupped his hard cock. She grinned when he moaned.

"You could throw me into an ice bath, and I'd still be hard when you're around."

"Now I'm rather tempted to test that theory."

Aaron growled, punishing her by nipping at her bottom lip. His tongue delved inside, and he sucked on her tongue in a way that made Alex shiver from head to toe. Damn, the man knew how to kiss.

"Tell me you want this," he growled.

"Aaron, I'm in my underwear, I'm about to take your cock out. What do you think? And bonus: I have a condom. Actually, I have an entire box."

Alex turned and opened the bottom drawer of her nightstand, pulling out a large box of condoms. Aaron's mouth twitched.

"How much sex were you planning on having?" he said.

"It was on sale. Besides, we'll probably need it."

He shook his head, laughing, and then Alex felt him unhook her bra, his callused fingers playing with her sensitive nipples. His touch was gentle, yet there was a feeling like he was claiming her with every stroke of his fingers.

"You're not going to freak out on me this time?" Aaron whispered the words against her throat.

"I hope not. I'm so horny, it's ridiculous."

That made him smile. "Are you already wet for me? I've barely gotten started."

Before Alex knew it, she was on the bed, her panties on

the floor with Aaron's head in between her legs. When he licked her core, she arched her hips, desperate for more.

He played with her until she was begging for release. His touch, his kiss—both combined to drive her to heights she'd never reached before. She'd had good sex, but this?

This was something else entirely.

When she was near to her release, he stopped, and she moaned in frustration. He just grinned and grabbed a condom.

"I want to feel you come around my cock," he growled.

Alex nearly came from those words alone.

When he finally thrust inside her, they both groaned, their voices joining together with every thrust of Aaron's hips. Alex dug her nails into his shoulders as his pace quickened. She could feel herself getting tighter and tighter, her orgasm within reach.

Even as he pounded into her, Aaron kissed her with a gentleness that nearly undid her. "Come for me, baby," he whispered. "I want to feel you."

Alex came in endless shudders of ecstasy, and Aaron wasn't far behind. He swallowed her yell with his mouth, groaning when his release made him shiver and shake.

Alex was boneless afterward; she felt like a rag doll. Aaron cleaned them both up and then spooned with her as the little spoon. The warmth of his body, the protection of his strong arms, made Alex feel like she could cry at any moment.

I think I'm falling in love with him, she thought. Even scarier, the thought didn't send her into a complete tailspin. It just made her feel content, even excited.

They didn't say much, both of them dozing for a time.

Alex had no intention of ever getting out of this bed if she could avoid it.

Eventually, she turned over to face Aaron. His expression was soft. She touched his hair and smiled.

"Hullo," he said.

"Hello to you."

He rubbed her arm, then moved to rub her neck. Alex closed her eyes and sighed happily.

"My brain keeps telling me I should regret what we just did," said Aaron, his voice quiet, "but I can't seem to find the energy."

Alex's eyes popped open. "*Do* you regret it?"

"No. My only regret is that I resisted you for so long."

"I do always get my way, in the end." She grinned. "Admit it. I won this round."

Aaron rolled his eyes, giving her a firm slap on the ass that made her yelp. "I'd argue that we both lost. You were just as resistant to this as I was."

"Only because you pissed me off so much."

"And now?"

"Well, do I seem mad?" Alex reached down and squeezed his cock, which was still half-hard. "This guy has made up for a lot."

"You're a brat."

Even as he said the words, Aaron kissed her, and then he was putting on another condom and plunging inside her until Alex saw stars for a second time.

After the second session, Aaron didn't cuddle her. He began to get dressed, wincing when he remembered that his clothes were still wet.

"I can put those in the dryer for you," Alex offered.

Aaron shook his head. "I need to get back home."

Alex sat up. She watched him dress, rather sad that he had to cover up such a delicious body. "So this was just a booty call?"

Grinning, he gave her a smacking kiss. "What else did you think it was?"

Alex hit him with a pillow, which would've turned into a wrestling match, but Aaron seemed to have regained his self-control. Once he was dressed, Alex realized he really was leaving.

Putting on a robe, she walked him to her door. Now she felt unsure.

"You're frowning at me," he commented.

"Was this just a one-off thing? Because I'd rather you tell me now than ghost me later."

Aaron brushed the hair away from her forehead. "No. I don't want it to be a one-off thing. Do you?"

Alex swallowed, her mouth dry. "No. I don't want that, either."

"Good."

He kissed her, and she felt tipsy from the taste of him. How had this man found a way into her heart so easily?

AARON CAME to Alex's as often as he was able. It was difficult, considering both of their work schedules and the kids.

Felicity, for her part, had yet to decide if she was moving out of the apartment completely. When Alex had asked

Gwen if she had any updates, Gwen had shaken her head, saying that Felicity wasn't sure yet.

Alex felt guilty that Felicity being gone meant that she and Aaron could be together. But even as she felt guilty, she couldn't tell him to stay away. Every time he knocked on her door and she opened it to see his face, it was like the sun peeking through the clouds after a rainy day.

One evening when Pen and Logan were at friends' houses, Aaron stayed the entire night for the first time. After they'd made love, they snuggled on the couch and watched movies.

"I don't get why you love rom-coms," Aaron was saying. "You already know how it's going to end."

"It's not about the ending. It's about the journey," replied Alex primly.

He looked skeptical, which meant that Alex made him watch some of her favorite rom-coms, including *When Harry Met Sally* and *How to Lose a Guy in 10 Days*.

When the credits began to roll, Aaron said suddenly, "My brother loved rom-coms."

Alex stilled. "Your brother?"

Aaron's mouth twisted into a sad smile. "He was a total sucker for them. You'd never think it, looking at him. But watch something romantic with him, and he'd be shedding tears by the end."

"That's adorable."

"He always told me after he'd had kids, he cried way more often. It was like a faucet had been turned on."

"So does that mean you cry more often?"

Aaron looked thoughtful. "Sometimes I *want* to, but it just doesn't happen. I've never been a crier, I guess." His voice was low when he admitted, "I didn't even cry at my brother's funeral."

Alex stilled. Aaron's jaw was clenched, and she could feel the confusion, the sadness, in his words. Her heart hurt.

"Did you cry later on?" she asked softly.

Aaron shook his head. "No. It doesn't make any sense, I know. I've never told anyone that."

"Sometimes, I guess, things hurt too much. Like you're frozen and can't cry." Alex sighed. "Then again, I'm a crier, so I probably have no idea what I'm talking about."

"Maybe men just don't cry like women do."

At that statement, Alex rolled her eyes. "You just said that your brother was a crier, so don't tell me men can't cry. I've seen my dad cry many times." She poked Aaron in the arm. "I bet I could find a movie that would make you cry."

"Doubtful. But you can try." His expression became faraway. "I always wanted to be just like my brother growing up. But I never thought I'd literally have to *be* him, you know? And I'm fucking it all up."

"I'm sure you're doing the best you can. You could've been a jerk and not taken in your niece and nephew. It takes a special kind of person to take on that kind of responsibility."

Now he looked annoyed. "I don't deserve a cookie for basic human decency. Besides, they're my family. I know you'd do the same for yours."

"My mom walked out on her own kids without a second glance. Maybe I could do the same thing." Even as Alex said the words, she felt sick to her stomach.

"Now you're talking bullshit." Aaron cupped her face, forcing her to meet his gaze. "I wouldn't be attracted to you if I thought you were the type of person who'd abandon the ones she loved. I've heard you talk about your sister and your dad."

Alex pushed his hand away. "I love them, but I can be selfish. Haven't you heard that from my sister?" She let out a mirthless laugh. "I bought the bookstore when I knew, deep down, it was a money sink. I caused Jocelyn stress, and my dad, because I couldn't help her with his bills. It was only Luke coming to the rescue that kept our dad out of a nursing home."

Alex knew she sounded bitter, but despite everything, she could feel that Aaron wasn't judging her. Just like she hadn't judged him with his earlier confession.

"Is that why you want to save the place?" His words were soft. "To prove your sister wrong?"

"Maybe. Probably," she conceded.

"It's not selfish to have ambition. What if the bookstore had turned out to be profitable? Sometimes business is just about luck. I've experienced it myself."

Alex shrugged. "Jocelyn doesn't believe in luck."

They fell silent for a time, and Alex wondered if Aaron had fallen asleep. But he began to rub her shoulders, and she realized how tense she was after their conversation.

"What is it with you and Jocelyn?" asked Aaron. "She warned me away from you, you know."

Alex whipped her head around. "What? She did?"

"She basically threatened to cut off my balls if I hurt you."

"Oh my God." Alex groaned, covering her face. "I'm so sorry. I did not tell her to do that! God, she always gets involved with things that are none of her business."

"She's protective of her little sister. I can't fault her for that."

"No, she's bossy, and domineering, and *controlling*—"

Aaron was rubbing her back now. "Down, girl. I wouldn't have told you if it made you this upset."

"I'm not upset with you. But I'm going to strangle Jocelyn." Forcing back her anger, she explained. "She has a history of meddling. So I tend to get really angry whenever she does it."

When Alex didn't explain further, Aaron turned her face toward him. "Tell me?" he asked.

Although Alex didn't really want to delve into this subject, she eventually began to tell Aaron about her relationship with Jocelyn. She recounted how it was growing up, and then told him how the Devon saga had pushed them nearly to the brink.

Aaron had said nothing during Alex's recital, and she couldn't help but wonder if he was judging her now.

"I don't always make the best decisions, as you can tell," said Alex, trying to sound lighthearted and failing.

Aaron had stopped touching her, and Alex suddenly felt like he was a million miles away.

Then, he said in a deceptively soft voice: "If Devon lived here still, I'd kill him myself."

Alex blinked. "What?"

"If he still lived in the state of Washington. No, the entire country. Hell, if he were in Antarctica, I'd find him and kill him for you."

Alex couldn't believe the words coming out of Aaron's mouth right then. The strangest part was that she believed him.

"Devon was a jerk, but I was also an idiot," she said.

"No, he took advantage of you. He manipulated you, pushed your boundaries. He was an adult."

"He was only eighteen, not fifty."

Aaron scowled. "I don't care. If a guy that age got near Pen..." He growled. "Well, let's just say it wouldn't end well."

Alex snuggled against Aaron's chest, petting him until the tension began to dissolve from his body. "You're cute when you get protective."

He harrumphed, which made her laugh. Then she brought his head down for a soft kiss.

"What was that for?" he asked.

She smiled, blinking away tears, her heart full to bursting. "No reason. I just like kissing you."

CHAPTER EIGHTEEN

Aaron had been worried that going out on a family outing for a Christmas tree and inviting Alex to come along would end poorly. Yet as he watched Pen chatter about all kinds of things with Alex, Logan inserting his own comments at random, Aaron realized his anxiety hadn't been necessary.

"Did you even have the Internet when you were our age?" asked Logan as the quartet wandered the Christmas tree farm.

Alex laughed. "I remember a time when we *didn't* have the Internet. We'd have to look things up in books, at the library. You know, like encyclopedias?"

Logan shook his head. "I don't like books."

"That's not something to be proud of," said Pen.

Logan shrugged and then ran off toward the other side of the farm.

It was a chilly day in early December, the skies gray but not threatening rain at the moment. When Aaron had asked

Alex if she'd wanted to come along to help them find a Christmas tree, he'd expected her to decline. But she'd accepted happily. Based on her expression, she seemed to fit right in.

"You know, we never had a real tree growing up," Alex was saying to Pen. "We always had a fake one."

Aaron was aghast. "You've never had a real Christmas tree?"

"Why do you sound like I just admitted that we never had food or water?" Alex's lips twitched.

Aaron gestured at the trees, the heady scent of pine bringing back all kinds of holiday memories. "Jason and I would help our dad find a tree to cut down," he explained. "But we once made the mistake of cutting down one that was too big, and our dad made us drag it back home anyway. Suffice to say our mom was not happy about us bringing an eight-foot tree to her doorstep."

Pen was listening intently. "Dad never told us that story."

"He'd probably blocked it from his memory. I'm pretty sure he complained about dragging the tree the entire way." Aaron grinned over at Alex. "I, though? I never once complained."

Alex rolled her eyes. "Sure, of course not. How old were you?"

"Probably seven?"

Alex just laughed at him, which made his chest feel tight. In her puffy down jacket and red beanie, her cheeks as red as her hat, Alex looked especially kissable right now. He had the sudden urge to wrap her braid around his wrist and pull her close—

"Uncle Aaron! Look at this one!" Logan called, breaking through Aaron's reverie.

Aaron shot Alex an amused look. "What do you want to bet he's found the tallest tree here?"

"Oh, without a doubt. You'll be dragging home another eight-foot tree if you're not careful," replied Alex.

Logan had, indeed, found the biggest tree on the farm. Aaron estimated it to be close to ten feet tall.

"Bud, our house is not big enough for a tree like this. We don't have ridiculously tall ceilings," said Aaron.

Logan got that look on his face that Aaron knew meant he was about to dig his heels in. "Yeah, we do! It'd totally fit in the living room."

"Logan, it's way too big," Pen said, sounding annoyed.

Logan's expression turned mulish. "You don't know that. You're just saying that because I found the best one before you did."

Pen sniffed, replying in a haughty voice that only a teenage girl could perfect, "I don't care which tree we get."

"Hey, wait, wait," interjected Alex, her voice rising above the kids'. "Let's ask somebody for a tape measure to see how tall it really is."

"How are we going to measure a tree twice our height?" Aaron asked.

Alex shrugged. "We'll figure it out. Logan, come on, let's find somebody and ask them. Maybe they know how tall all of the trees are already."

Logan looked uncertain, but to Aaron's surprise, he followed Alex without protest. What magic spell had she cast on his usually obstinate nephew?

By the end of the visit, they'd determined that Logan's

tree was, in fact, too tall, but Alex helped him find another one that was even better. It was lusher—Pen named it Fat Tree—and was just the right height for their living room.

"You're sure this is the one you want?" asked Aaron. "Because we're not coming back if you change your mind."

Logan nodded his head, while Pen shrugged a single shoulder, which Aaron translated to *I'm not going to show you that I care but I do.*

After they'd bought and then strapped Fat Tree to the roof of Aaron's car, he gave the kids some money to go buy them all apple cider at a nearby booth.

"You were good with them," said Aaron, trying to sound casual.

"I guess I remember what I was like at that age. Logan reminds me of myself. Well, so does Pen. They're good kids."

Aaron watched as the two siblings began squabbling over the money and let out a tired laugh. "I'm not so sure I'm doing the best by them, though."

"What do you mean?"

"I mean, I'm not their dad. I'll never replace him. I'm flying by the seat of my pants here, and sometimes I wonder if that'll hurt them in the end."

Alex was silent for a long moment, which only made Aaron feel desperate for her to say something.

"I can't imagine what you all have gone through," she began, her voice soft. "But you're still their family. You took them in, and you care enough to do right by them. That counts for something. Nobody is perfect at parenting."

"I don't care about being perfect. I care that I'm not completely screwing them up."

"Aaron, you're *here*." Alex squeezed his forearm. "My mom? She wasn't here. She left and basically disappeared from our lives. Our dad, though, he stayed. He raised us. He didn't do the best job ever. But at the end of the day, kids need love. That's it."

"You make it sound so simple."

"I think you're making things more complicated than they need to be."

Gazing down into her dark eyes, Aaron couldn't help but lean down to kiss her. Pen and Logan were still facing away from them, but even if they saw Aaron kissing Alex, Aaron wouldn't care.

Alex returned the kiss, until everything around them melted away. It was only the sound of Logan's voice that forced Aaron to break away.

"What was that for?" Alex's eyes were bright and shining.

"Because you're beautiful," he said simply.

Alex opened her mouth to reply, but the kids were upon them and telling them all about buying the cider. Apparently, the customer ahead of them had been upset that there were no options for adding booze to the cider.

"She was so mad," said Logan, clearly relishing the experience. "She threw her money at the guy at the counter. It was crazy."

"She didn't *throw* it," said Pen, exasperated. "He just wasn't paying attention when she tried to give him her money."

"She totally threw it! You didn't see it. You were looking at some bird."

The conversation quickly descended into a squabble

that continued into the car. It was only Alex telling them ridiculous stories of customers behaving badly at the bookstore that stopped the argument.

"I once had this guy come in every morning," Alex was saying, "and he'd stay for like an hour. Sometimes two. He'd never buy anything, though. One day, I followed him around the store, because I had a feeling he was shoplifting or something."

"You just had a feeling?" asked Aaron, skeptical.

"If you've ever worked retail, you can tell. Also, he always brought in a giant bag. Anyway, one day, I was watching him. He'd picked up a book and was reading it aloud to himself, which I thought was strange. Then I realized that there was something in the bag—"

"Was it a dog?" interjected Logan. "A cat? What was it?"

Alex shot Aaron an amused look. "Wrong, and wrong."

The kids threw out other answers, all of them wrong.

Finally, Alex said, "It was a raccoon."

"What? No way," said Logan.

Pen was frowning. "A pet raccoon?"

Alex held up her hand. "I swear it. He had a pet raccoon in his bag and was reading stories to it. When he saw me watching, though, he stopped and never returned to the store." Alex sighed. "Too bad. I wanted to meet his raccoon."

"I want a raccoon. They're so cute," said Pen. "Uncle Aaron, can we get one?"

"What? No. They're not pets. Besides, they have rabies." Aaron shot Alex a look. "Right? They aren't pets."

"Anything can be a pet if you want it to be," was her

reply, which then sparked another conversation about what wild animal you'd most like to have for a pet.

Logan wanted a rhino. Pen, an ocelot. Alex wanted a river otter, while Aaron just said that he'd rather not have a wild animal as a pet at all.

"Boring," said Alex, sticking out her tongue. "It's hypothetical, Aaron. Come on, what's your favorite animal?"

After some more pressure from everyone else, Aaron conceded that he'd most like to have a capybara as a pet.

Pen made a face at this pronouncement. "Isn't that a giant rat?"

"Have you ever watched capybara videos? They're the chillest animals ever. Look it up," said Aaron.

The kids began searching for videos of capybaras, but even after watching a few, neither were convinced. "That's a weird choice," said Logan.

"Yeah, Uncle Aaron. Only you would want a giant rat as a pet," joked Alex.

"You want a river otter!"

"Otters aren't rodents." This came from Pen. She sounded like she was concerned Aaron was a little slow.

When they arrived at Alex's apartment, Aaron got out of the car to walk her to her door. "Thank you for coming today," he said. "I know it was kind of chaotic."

"I had a nice time. I liked getting to know your niece and nephew. I see a lot of you in them."

Aaron blinked in surprise. "Really? Like what?"

"Well, you're just as stubborn as Logan. Don't give me that look, you are. Also, you and Pen make the same face when somebody says something weird. It's cute."

Aaron leaned in and kissed her, keeping the kiss brief

since the kids were probably watching them. They said goodbye, and Aaron returned to the car, feeling like he was walking on air.

It didn't take long for Logan to pop Aaron's bubble. He was sniggering under his breath, like he'd found out an embarrassing secret. Pen was studiously not looking at Aaron.

"What, Logan?" said Aaron, exasperated.

"You were *kissing*. We saw you," said Logan.

"Yes, that happens sometimes. Didn't you see your parents kiss?"

Pen screwed up her face. "Gross. Don't talk about that."

Logan then asked, "Are you guys together now? What happened to the other lady? The blonde?"

Aaron grimaced. "Felicity and I just didn't work out."

"So are you going to marry Alex?" asked Logan.

Aaron mustered a straight face, but his voice was tight as he told his nephew no.

But the thought of marrying Alex, of making her a part of their family, would not leave Aaron's mind the rest of the afternoon. Even as they set up the Christmas tree and began stringing the lights, Aaron couldn't stop imagining it.

What would Alex be like as a mother? Initially, Aaron had assumed she would be more of the fun parent and nothing else. He realized he'd underestimated her. Or more likely, he'd told himself she wouldn't suit to give himself a reason to stay away from her.

As Aaron watched Pen and Logan hang ornaments, Aaron wished he'd invited Alex to do this activity. Most of all, he wanted her around—always. The thought both excited and terrified him.

They'd gotten off to a rocky start. But what if they could make it work? It was the one instance where Aaron would be glad to be proven wrong.

CHAPTER NINETEEN

I t was the first night Alex would stay the night at Aaron's place. Both kids were at friends' houses. Aaron warned Alex that unless she wanted to run into them in the morning, though, she should probably head out early.

"Are you telling me that you're kicking me out at dawn?" she joked as she took in the Christmas tree.

Aaron came up behind her, hugging her from behind. "I'm just trying to protect you from annoying preteen comments."

"They know we're..." Alex struggled to choose the right word. "Seeing each other?"

"You went shopping for this tree with us."

"Doesn't mean they don't think I'm just a friend."

Aaron kissed her neck, his hands roving over her body. It only took a few touches, a few kisses, and she was putty in his hands.

Stepping away, she pointed at one of the ornaments, an ugly-looking thing that looked like a bird. Except it was missing a head.

"What happened here?" she asked.

"When Pen was little, she thought it was a cookie." Aaron held up the ornament, which did, in fact, look like a cookie. Except this cookie was rock-hard. "She nearly broke a tooth on it, if I remember correctly."

"Poor thing. I would've thought the same thing."

"My brother loved telling that story. It's also why we kept the ornament. The headless goose ornament, courtesy of Pen."

Alex could tell he was far away, thinking of happier times. Alex returned the ornament to its previous spot. She asked Aaron about a few other ornaments, but she could soon tell that talking about his brother and sister-in-law was making him look pensive.

"I wish I could have met them," said Alex. "They sounded like amazing people."

Aaron was staring down at a *Just Married* ornament, brushing his thumb across the date. "They were. They were the best people."

"I'm sure they're looking down on you, happy that you're the one taking care of their kids."

Aaron shook his head. "Maybe. Or they're jealous that it's me, and not them."

"There's no such thing as jealousy in heaven, you heathen."

Aaron's eyes sparked, and Alex was soon giggling as he yanked her into his arms. "Oh, so you mean I couldn't do this to you?" he said, cupping her breasts.

"No lust in heaven," she murmured.

"That's a damn shame. I love that particular vice."

He reached under her sweater, his expression turning predatory when he discovered she wasn't wearing a bra.

"I appreciate the easy access," he said, grinning as he rubbed her nipples.

Alex licked her lips. "I didn't do it for you." Even as she said the words, she could hear the lie in them.

"Even so, I appreciate it just the same."

They kissed for a while longer, touching and playing, but then Alex's stomach rumbled so loudly that they both laughed.

"I guess I should feed you first. You'll need your strength for tonight," said Aaron.

Alex didn't doubt he spoke the truth.

Aaron ordered them a pizza—he told her his cooking was abysmal—and they spent the evening eating, drinking, and laughing. Alex put her feet in Aaron's lap, and he obliged her and rubbed her feet. When she started to get too sleepy, though, he'd start tickling the soles until she begged for mercy.

They eventually found their way upstairs to his bedroom. It contained only a king-sized bed, a tiny dresser, and a box that functioned as a nightstand. Alex took in the decor, amused.

"You couldn't spring for a nightstand?" she joked.

Aaron shrugged. "Haven't taken the time to get one."

She couldn't help but inspect his closet, where a handful of pants and shirts hung in neat rows.

"I don't keep the bodies in there," he said over her shoulder.

Alex snickered. "Of course not. They're in the crawl space under the house, right?"

"Oh, you're too clever for me."

Aaron wrapped his arms around her, kissing her and licking inside her mouth. Alex let herself be seduced, slowly and thoroughly. Aaron seemed to touch every inch of her body.

He worshipped her: with his mouth, his hands. He told her she was beautiful and that her skin was the silkiest he'd ever felt. When he took a nipple into his mouth and sucked, Alex nearly came right then and there.

But Alex didn't want to just be the receiver. She stripped Aaron of his jeans and boxers, palming his half-hard cock until it was rigid under her fingers. Aaron watched her face the entire time as she squeezed and stroked his length.

When she kneeled at his feet, he didn't say a word. Instead, he tangled his hand in her hair and let her have her fun.

She licked his cock, tasting him. When she took him inside her mouth, she could feel him shudder.

"You're amazing," he groaned. "God, your mouth—"

She sucked harder, and she smiled when his grip tightened in her hair.

But even as she felt him getting closer to orgasm, he stopped her, pulling her up for a bruising kiss. Then they were falling onto his bed, and after he hurriedly put on a condom, he thrust hard inside her.

Alex gasped, and her gasps continued as he pounded into her. Their movements made his bed squeak, the headboard bouncing off the wall. Alex would've made a joke about it, but then Aaron was moving so she was on her hands and knees in front of him.

She buried her face in the comforter. With every thrust

of his hips, he sent her to new heights. She felt like she was going to catapult straight out of her body with every stroke of his cock inside her.

She felt herself tighten until it was nearly painful. And when her release hit her, she screamed into the sheets, her entire body writhing in ecstasy.

Aaron wasn't far behind her. He grunted, and with his fingers digging into her hips, she felt his cock flex as he came. She gave him another hip wiggle that elicited a grunt from him.

He collapsed next to her, both of them sweaty and breathless. Alex wondered if her bones had melted. It certainly felt like they had.

Aaron brushed her hair from her forehead. "How are you?"

"Pretty good. Yourself?"

"I'm fucking fantastic."

She laughed, and he kissed her. Then he was touching her, squeezing her ass, kissing her neck. She couldn't believe she'd want him again so soon, but clearly she was insatiable.

They fell asleep in each other's arms. Alex awoke to darkness, and it took her a moment to remember where she was.

Aaron was snoring softly next to her. Gently untangling her limbs from his, she went to the bathroom and washed up. By the time she returned, Aaron was awake again.

"Doing okay?" he asked her as she got back into bed.

"I mean, I just had to pee. Unless you want a play-by-play of my time in the bathroom?"

He tweaked her chin. "No, I'm good. Thanks for offering, though."

Alex sighed, cuddling into his embrace. He was so warm, and she shivered as her sensitive nipples brushed against his chest hair. Over the course of the weeks they'd been together, she'd discovered that he only had a smattering of chest hair that led to a blond happy trail. She'd also discovered that he had three moles on his back, that he wasn't ticklish anywhere, and that he purred like a cat when she sifted her fingers through his hair.

She did so now, gently scratching his scalp, and he moaned as she petted him.

"Sometimes I wonder if you're more dog than human," she said with a grin.

"When you do that, I can't even disagree." He sighed happily.

Alex thought he'd fallen asleep again, but then he said out of the blue, "I never thought this would happen."

"What? Me scratching your head?"

He grunt-laughed. "No, this. Us, together, in my bed. After that kiss we had on the beach, I thought I'd never see you again. And then when I did, and you hated me—"

"I never *hated* you."

Alex could feel his gaze on her. "Now, that's the biggest lie I've ever heard," he said.

"You just pissed me off. There's a difference."

"Hmm." He didn't sound convinced. "At any rate, I'm glad you're here. I also don't want you to think that I'm trying to hide you from the kids, either."

Alex swallowed, her mouth suddenly dry. "What are you getting at?"

Sighing, Aaron rolled onto his back. "When Jason and Ashley died and the kids came to live with me, I knew my dating life was going to be nonexistent, at least for a while. It also wouldn't be fair to bring in a woman who might not stick around, you know?"

Alex's heart was pounding now, and suddenly she felt cold, even next to Aaron and covered with blankets. "That makes sense," she whispered.

"What I'm saying is, I made an assumption, but I was wrong. I think we could make this thing work. We could make it real."

Alex suddenly felt like the room was unbearably small. "You're assuming I want the same thing," she replied.

"I mean, I'm asking. Do you? Because I want to date you. For real. And then see where this thing goes. Maybe it'll turn into something more. Isn't that a possibility you've considered?"

"No, not really." Alex bent down, trying to find her clothes in the dark and failing miserably. Grunting, she finally turned on the overhead light that made them both blink. "I should head out."

Rumpled and delicious, Aaron somehow looked handsome even under the harshness of the overhead light. "It's the middle of the night," he said.

"Or just really early in the morning. Depends on how you look at it."

Alex felt less exposed with every garment she donned. By the time she was dressed, though, Aaron had risen—naked—from the bed and taken her by the arms.

"Why are you freaking out on me?" he asked. "I thought you'd be happy about this."

"You're making a lot of assumptions about me tonight."

"I'm trying to get you to answer the damn question!"

Alex's chin rose. "No, you're plowing ahead without even wanting to hear what I have to say. If I told you that I wanted to keep things casual, would you hear me? Or would you just keep trying to persuade me otherwise? Because I've been in a relationship like that before, and I'm not interested in doing it a second time."

Aaron looked stunned. "Are you seriously comparing me to your shitty high school boyfriend?"

"I tend to date men who aren't good for me. I think they're amazing, until they show that they just want to control my every move."

Aaron's fingers dug into her forearms. "I'm not trying to control you, dammit!"

Alex pushed his hands away. "You're doing a shit job of convincing me. Look, I know you were looking for the perfect woman to be your wife and the kids' new mom, all in one. But I'm not that paragon of a woman. So stop trying to force me into a role I never asked for."

Aaron's face was flushed now, and Alex was surprised to see that he was nearly shaking with anger. Fear made Alex step away from him. He saw it, and hurt slashed across his face.

"I'm not going to stop you from leaving," he said. "You've always been free to make your own choices."

Alex smiled grimly. "Thank you? I guess."

"You're not thinking clearly, you know. Let me know when you come to your senses again."

Alex gaped at him. "Wow, way to be a condescending douche. I'm out. Happy? I'm going home, and you'll never have to hear from me again."

Alex half-expected him to follow her out to her car, but

he didn't. He didn't say a word as she grabbed her bag. And he didn't even come to his window to watch her drive off. She made sure to look, just in case.

CHAPTER TWENTY

After countless back-and-forth emails and a previous cancellation, it was finally the day of Lila White's signing at the bookstore. Alex threw herself into preparations, excitement filling her when the boxes of books were delivered.

"How many preorders did we get?" Chris asked, his eyes widening as box after box was wheeled inside.

"I lost count. I also might have bought a bunch for anyone who didn't preorder," said Alex.

By the time the boxes were all delivered, completely filling the small storage space in the back, Alex felt like she was on cloud nine.

Surely, she thought, this would give them enough wiggle room to get through the next quarter. Maybe even the one after that. The thought of shocking Aaron by paying the increased rent... It was enough to make her do a dance throughout the store.

She and Chris worked through the day and through the evening the Friday before the event. She apologized multiple times to Chris, telling him she'd give him a huge bonus if she could.

"You're lucky I like you," said Chris. He yawned widely. "God, I'm getting to the point that if I see another Lila White book I might scream. I swear I had a nightmare about one last night."

Alex held up the author's latest release and joked, "I'm going to haunt your dreams, Chris! Oooowwooooooo!"

"If you're trying to sound like a ghost, stop. You sound like a dying dog."

They both went home exhausted, only getting a few hours of sleep. The morning of the signing, Alex arrived an hour before Chris, setting up any last-minute items like extra chairs, more pens on the signing table, and a stack of books close by. Books were behind the register as well, along with in the window. The entire store had been transformed for the event.

According to Lila's publicist, she would arrive by ten a.m., the signing starting an hour later. Alex had never met the woman in person. The little communication she'd had was through her publicist. And unlike most authors, Lila didn't have much of a presence online besides a website. No author photos, either.

But Alex figured she just preferred to keep her life private. Alex couldn't blame her. She'd seen enough social media shenanigans to know that she'd be hesitant to put herself out there if the opportunity presented itself.

The bookstore started to fill before ten a.m. By the time the clock struck ten, Alex was busily getting people their preordered books and checking them out at the register.

"Um, boss," said Chris over her shoulder. "It's half past ten."

"Yeah, and?"

"Um. She said ten, right?"

Alex smiled at the girl in front of her. "Excuse us," she said, taking Chris aside and hustling them both into her office. "Let me check my email. Maybe there's a reason why she's running late..."

But Alex's inbox was empty. She quickly sent an email to Alex's publicist, but she doubted she'd get a reply on a Saturday.

"You don't have Lila's number? Can you text her?" asked Chris.

"I couldn't even find the woman's picture. You think I got her *number*?"

"I mean, that doesn't seem like a huge ask."

Alex tried calling the publicist, but she got a voicemail. She glanced at the clock on the wall: it was now a quarter till eleven.

"Well, maybe she missed the ferry and is running late. We'll just have to hope she shows up soon," said Alex. She tried to sound unconcerned, but based on Chris' expression, he didn't buy it.

By eleven a.m., Alex's stomach was twisting. By eleven thirty, she stood in front of the gathered crowd, a crowd that now snaked around the building.

She said in a voice that belied her rising panic, "Ms. White should be here shortly. She got caught in traffic. I'm so sorry for the wait!"

Alex was grateful that almost everyone was understanding and willing to wait. But as the minutes ticked by, as

Alex called the publicist over and over again, as her inbox remained terrifyingly empty, Alex had a sinking suspicion that Lila White had ghosted her.

Alex gave it until noon. At that point, a number of people had already left. The crowd was restless, and they were asking questions that Alex and Chris couldn't answer. Poor Chris at one point had to hide out in Alex's office to escape.

Alex herself had to go to her office, take a deep breath, and force back the tears that threatened to spring forth any moment. She wondered if she was going to be sick.

"Everyone," she said, standing once again at the empty signing table, "I'm afraid to tell you that the signing has been canceled due to unforeseen events. I'm so very sorry."

"Are we getting ticket refunds?" a woman in the front demanded. "I came all the way from Seattle for this."

"I came from Portland!" another woman said. A third said that she'd flown in from Los Angeles. San Francisco, Las Vegas. Even as far as Texas.

Alex thought of all the lost money from giving refunds and was sure she was going to vomit in front of everyone. "As you can see, our store is small, and we don't have a large staff. But I'll be issuing refunds to everyone in the coming days. Please be patient as we get to everyone."

That pronouncement seemed to settle the crowd, but not completely. Alex was hounded with questions the rest of the day, demanding to know if Lila had even been scheduled to appear at all. It had taken all of Alex's self-control not to snap back at the insinuation that she'd led hundreds of people on.

"Hi, Alex," said a voice from behind Alex.

Alex turned to see Pen holding Lila White's latest against her chest. "So she's not coming?" the teenager asked.

"No, she's not." Alex winced inwardly at the tone of her voice, but then she was pulled away before she could apologize.

The last of the eventgoers didn't leave until after three p.m. By then, both Alex and Chris were exhausted, sweaty, and their voices were hoarse from talking.

"I'm going to close up early," said Alex. "You can go home. And take tomorrow off, too. You've more than earned it."

"What about you? You look like you're about to collapse." Chris shot her a worried look.

"I'll be okay. This is just a hiccup, right? I'll figure it out. Don't worry about it. Thank you for all of your hard work today. I wouldn't have gotten through it without you."

To Alex's surprise, Chris pulled her into a tight, quick hug. It took all of her strength not to burst into tears right then and there.

"I'm going home and drinking. You're welcome to join me," said Chris.

Alex's smile wobbled. "I might take you up on that."

But Alex needed time to be alone. After locking the front door, she went to her office, closed the door, and sat down before the tears started flowing.

It's all over, she thought in utter despair. *This was the one chance we had of turning the tide, but we failed.*

She thought of Aaron, and she wondered bitterly if he'd even be sad that the signing had turned into a disaster. He'd get his way in the end: he'd force her out and get the tenant he wanted.

She had the wild thought that he'd been behind this, but she knew that was crazy. More than likely, it'd simply been a public figure who'd decided at the last minute not to attend her own signing.

When Alex's phone rang and she saw it was Lila's publicist, she let it go to voicemail. Alex didn't want an explanation. Sure, maybe Lila had had some emergency, but Alex had the sinking feeling she'd simply ghosted her. *Again.*

"Fool me once, shame on you," muttered Alex to herself. "Fool me twice, shame on me."

WHEN PEN CAME HOME and told Aaron about the signing, he waited until the store was closed for the day and made his way to Alex's.

She didn't answer the door at his first knock. He knocked harder the second time, which a few moments later resulted in Alex slowly opening the door a crack.

"Alex," he said, "let me in."

"I'm tired, Aaron. Go home." Her voice cracked.

"Let me in," he said more firmly.

Sighing, she opened the door for him. She was wearing oversized sweatpants and a ripped-up tank, her hair in a messy bun. When Aaron saw her face, though, he froze.

Her eyes were red from crying. There were dark circles under her eyes, and she looked like she'd lost weight. It'd only been a week since he'd last seen her, yet she looked like a complete wreck.

"Yeah, I look like shit," she said. "I didn't think I'd have company."

He noticed she was drinking wine from a plastic tumbler. Based on how slowly she was walking, she was either drunk or exhausted. Probably both.

"I wanted to see how you were," he said.

She scoffed. "No, you didn't. You wanted to gloat."

"Gloat?" he repeated, stunned. "Over what?"

Alex tipped back her cup and finished it in one gulp. "Oh, come on. You know what this means. The store is kaput. Dunzo. You think I can pay that hefty rent increase now? No fucking way. Well, congrats. You won."

"You think I came here because I'm happy about all of this? Give me some credit."

"You know, I thought for a second you were behind Lila not coming, but even you aren't that devious. No, I just have notoriously bad luck. Or I am just an impulsive moron." Alex shrugged. "I knew getting with you was a mistake, but guess what? I did it anyway." She let out a bitter laugh.

Aaron grabbed hold of her arms, mostly to steady her. Her pupils were blown out, and he pressed a hand to her forehead. "You're burning up," he said.

"I'm drunk, sweetheart. That happens when you drink."

"You also don't know what you're saying. I'll come back when you've slept it off—"

"You really think you can just wave a magic wand, and everything will be fine?" She shook her head. "Your arrogance is impressive, honestly. You think something is yours and it'll just fall into your lap. Well, I'm not a thing you're just going to claim for your own."

He wanted to shake her. His carefully leashed anger

fought to be freed. He knew Alex was lashing out. He knew it, but it didn't make him feel better about it.

"I care about you," said Aaron, his voice low, "and I want you to see that we could be good together. We could make a life together. Is that so wrong? Does that make me controlling?"

Alex struggled to free herself from his grip. He let her go, albeit reluctantly.

"And then what? You'll make me into the perfect house-wife who does everything you say? I'll close the store and take care of your kids because you just can't do it? No way. No way in hell. I know what you thought you wanted from Felicity, but I am not her—"

"You think I don't know that? I don't want to change you. Christ, how can you say that? Alex, listen to me. Don't do this. We have something, but you're throwing it away with both hands because you're scared."

Alex brought her chin up, the stubborn set of her mouth warning Aaron that she wasn't going to give in. "Don't tell me how I should feel."

Aaron was seething now. "Seriously? Stop twisting my fucking words! You're making me out to be the villain when, guess what? You've created this mess yourself. You bought that store knowing full and well that it was a money sink. I'm not going to apologize for doing what I need to do as your landlord. Stop taking your frustration out on me and take some fucking responsibility for once."

Alex's bottom lip was quivering. But she didn't shed a tear.

"Maybe buying it was a mistake, but I've been working my ass off to make things work. But you, you refused to budge. I should have known. At the end of the day, it's only about money with you. Did you ever care about me? Or did you just care about the bottom line?"

Aaron snarled, "Aren't you the one who made a deal with me? I scratch your back if you scratch mine. Or did you just sleep with me to get on my good side?"

"Ah, you've figured it out. I only had sex with you to get my rent lowered." She gave him a wobbly bow. "Now that you know, I'm going to bed. You can find your way out."

Aaron wanted to grab her again. He wanted to haul her into his arms, kiss her, make her admit that she cared. But he knew how stubborn she was. And he also knew that she'd probably never forgive him for what he'd said.

She looked over her shoulder at him. "I wanted you, full stop. I wanted you since that night on the beach. But I guess we weren't meant to be."

Aaron's heart shattered as she swiped away a tear and staggered down the hall to her bedroom without him.

ALL THOUGHTS of Alex fled when Aaron returned home to find Pen sitting in the kitchen, crying. In her hand was a piece of notebook paper.

"What is it? What happened?" he asked.

When she handed him the note, it took him a second to realize that it was in Logan's nearly illegible scrawl.

By the time Aaron read to the end, he felt numb. "When did you find this?" he asked Pen, his voice sounding far away.

"I don't know. I went to the bookstore for the signing,

and I thought he was in his room. But when I found it, you'd already left. I called you, but you didn't pick up." Her tone was accusatory.

Aaron checked his phone, discovering that he'd accidentally put it on silent. On the screen were multiple missed calls, all from Pen. Nothing from Logan.

Don't come looking for me, the note had read. It had essentially declared that Logan was running away, and nobody was going to stop him.

Aaron, thinking Logan might just be pranking them, went over the house from top to bottom. But Logan wasn't hiding anywhere.

When Aaron went into Logan's room and found that his backpack was gone, along with his favorite handheld video game, Aaron knew with a sinking feeling that Logan hadn't been joking at all.

CHAPTER TWENTY-ONE

While Aaron waited for the police to arrive, he paced the living room. Although every fiber of his being wanted to go searching for Logan, he knew he had to stay put for now.

Pen sat in the living room with him, saying nothing.

"Did he say anything to you?" Aaron asked. "Anything at all?"

Pen shook her head. "Sometimes he'd tell our dad that he'd run away, but that was a long time ago. One time he packed a bag, but when he found out he couldn't take his tablet with him, he changed his mind."

Aaron grunted out a laugh. "How old was he, then?"

"Six? I can't remember."

Aaron kept pacing. In the corner stood the Christmas tree, bright with lights, and he had the sudden urge to toss the damned thing out the window.

Why, Logan? he kept thinking to himself over and over. *Where are you?*

Aaron had called Logan's phone multiple times. He'd

texted. He'd even tried to track the phone's location, but Logan had apparently been smart enough to turn that feature off.

How had he known how to do that? And why hadn't Aaron thought to lock that feature so Logan couldn't change it?

This is why I should never have gotten custody, he thought grimly. *Jason, if you were here, this never would have happened.*

The police arrived quickly. They took Aaron's statement, and then Pen's. They asked all kinds of questions, including ones that made Aaron feel like the most neglectful parent who'd ever existed.

"You were gone from the house for how long?" Officer Klein, a middle-aged man with a bushy mustache, asked Aaron a second time. "Where were you while you were gone?"

Aaron glanced at Pen. "I don't see how that's relevant."

"Sir, we're gathering as much information as we can. Your cooperation would be appreciated."

After they'd gotten what they needed, the officers informed Aaron that since it seemed that Logan had run away of his own volition, they wouldn't be issuing an AMBER alert.

"He's a child," said Aaron, frustrated. "He's out there, God knows where, alone."

"He's a runaway," said the female officer, a young woman named Officer Layton. "In these situations, we generally find them within twenty-four hours. He's only eleven, right? He can't drive, and he'll probably draw attention for being a young kid by himself. He might also return home on his own."

Aaron's head was pounding. After thanking the officers, he pressed his forehead to the door, his mind racing.

"Uncle Aaron?" Pen's voice was soft. "Are we going to find Logan?"

Aaron turned and hugged Pen close. "Of course we are. He can't have gotten far."

SINCE IT WAS ALREADY dark outside, Aaron struggled not to panic. He called all of his contacts, along with all of Logan's friends and their parents. No one had seen him.

Aaron went to the school; he went to the park. He and Pen went up and down their street, Aaron using a flashlight from the car window to help illuminate the shadowy streets. When it started raining, it made visibility even worse.

Aaron's phone was alerting him so often with new texts that he made Pen the one to read him any updates. The only consolation in this situation was that the news of Logan's disappearance seemed to have spread across the island rapidly.

One of Aaron's neighbors hailed him from the sidewalk. "Any news?" she asked.

Aaron shook his head. "Nothing yet."

The night stretched on. Aaron took Pen home and continued the search. The island was only so big, and the only way off of it was to take the ferry. Multiple people had already searched the ferry station and hadn't seen Logan anywhere. Luke had texted Aaron that he'd stay at the station just in case Logan showed up there.

Aaron's stomach was in knots all night. What if Logan

had already taken a ferry to Seattle? If he were in the city, he'd be impossible to locate. Then again, wouldn't somebody notice a young kid wandering on his own?

Aaron wasn't sure if Logan even had any money. Then again, maybe Logan had stashed away a decent amount that Aaron had been unaware of.

A few miles from home, Aaron began walking down the length of Main Street. He went into every open restaurant, and flashed a light down every alley, calling for Logan until his voice went hoarse.

ALEX HAD FALLEN asleep when she heard her phone buzz. She ignored it, but then it kept buzzing. And buzzing.

"What in the world..." she muttered. When she finally read Jocelyn's text, though, she sprang from her bed and got dressed so quickly that she nearly fell flat on her face in her haste.

Logan Morrison ran away. Have you seen him? Jocelyn had texted.

Alex checked to see if Aaron had messaged her, but it had only been Jocelyn. Surely, even after their fight, he'd want everyone on the island helping him in the search?

She called Aaron. Voicemail. She called him a second time, and still, she got his voicemail.

She drove straight to Jocelyn and Luke's. Jocelyn was home, and she updated Alex with what she knew.

"Gwen, Felicity, and Jack are out searching," she told Alex.

"Do you know where they went?"

Jocelyn shook her head. "Call Gwen."

Alex had been avoiding Gwen, and by extension Felicity, but this was no time to be delicate.

And that was how Alex met up with Gwen at a park in the middle of the night.

Felicity gave Alex a brief hello while Gwen updated her on the situation as best as she could.

"It's chaotic right now. Everyone is talking to Aaron, but he's not giving everyone updates. So we don't know what places have been searched, what places need to be searched..." Gwen sighed. "I can't blame him. I'd be frantic."

Alex's heart hurt thinking about Aaron searching for Logan. Was he alone? Knowing him, he wouldn't have asked someone to stay with him.

"I need one of you to tell me where Aaron is," said Alex.

"You can't ask him yourself?" said Gwen, puzzled.

"He won't answer my calls." Alex grimaced. "We had a fight earlier. We said some things. But it doesn't matter now. Finding Logan is what matters."

Gwen glanced at Felicity, but Felicity's expression was neutral. And then Jack was striding toward them, telling them he hadn't seen Logan anywhere on the playground just yards away.

By the time Alex had gotten Aaron's location, she was the one frantic with worry. As she drove across the island, she realized in a flash of insight that she loved Aaron.

She loved him. And she'd destroyed any chance she had of their having a relationship.

Tears dripped down her face: of frustration, of heartbreak. Most of all, she hated herself. Why did she always have to destroy what was good in her life? She'd been so angry about Lila White not showing up, about losing the bookstore, that she'd lashed out at Aaron because he'd been a convenient target.

Don't think about that now, she told herself, wiping away the tears. *This is about finding Logan.*

Even as she told herself that, she still couldn't stop her heart from fluttering when she finally spotted Aaron. He was walking along the road, not far from the ferry station, the hood of his raincoat concealing his face.

Alex knew it was him, though. She'd recognize that walk anywhere. It also helped that she remembered that his raincoat was a bright green.

"Aaron!" She parked her car, not caring if she was parked legally or not, and sprinted over to Aaron. "Any news?"

Aaron didn't stop walking. Alex almost had to jog to keep up with his long stride. "What are you doing here?" he asked her gruffly.

"I didn't want you to be alone," she said.

He stopped walking; Alex nearly collided with his back.

Then he said, "You don't need to be here. You'd probably be better off looking somewhere else, anyway."

"Maybe, but you need somebody who can be the one to keep everyone else updated. Because as far as I can tell, you aren't doing a great job right now."

He turned toward her, a severe frown on his face. "Are you seriously criticizing me *now*?"

"I want to help you." She put her hands out, palms up. "I can be that point person so you don't have to think about it."

He stared at her. She had a feeling he wasn't sure if he should believe her or not. That hurt, but she couldn't blame him, either.

"I'm sorry," she blurted. "You have to know how sorry I am."

His expression softened slightly. "It doesn't matter. Not now." He thrust his phone into her hand and gave her the passcode. "I haven't seen the latest texts. It's too overwhelming to go through constantly."

Alex went to her car, mostly so she could see what she was doing, Aaron reluctantly sitting in the passenger seat. She rifled through her glove compartment for the paper map of the island that her dad had given her ages ago. She'd never used it since she had a smartphone. But in that moment, she was thankful she'd kept it.

She spread the map out for both her and Aaron to see. "We've searched here, here, and here," she said, circling each location. "Gwen is currently searching here, while Jack is here." She kept circling. "Where all have you looked?"

Aaron took the pen from her and started circling. They realized quickly that their searches were haphazard and covering the same ground. After some discussion, she and Aaron made a plan that would be more efficient and not duplicate any previous searches.

Alex not only sent a group text, but also started posting on social media. "The more people who see this, the better," she explained to Aaron.

Once the plan was in place, she and Aaron began sketching the bus route that Logan might've taken. They backtracked to the closest bus stop to Aaron's house. When the bus arrived, they questioned the driver, but he didn't have any information for them.

They continued with the next stop and the next driver, and by the fourth bus, they finally had a lead. That driver mentioned that he'd noticed Logan getting on the bus, as he'd hadn't enough money to pay his fare and the driver had let him board anyway.

"Where did he get off?" asked Aaron.

"Not sure. He got off through the back entrance, most likely. But you can take one of the route maps and see if that helps you."

Unfortunately, by the time they drove to the next stop, the buses had already stopped running for the night. Aaron swore, looking like he wanted to tear his hair out.

"I'm sorry," whispered Alex. She felt helpless.

"What if he's out there, in the cold and rain, wondering why we haven't found him yet?" Aaron's voice broke. "Or he's hurt somewhere? We might find him too late—"

"Stop. Don't do this to yourself. We'll find him. I know we will. He's a smart kid. You said so yourself."

Aaron took a deep breath. Then another. To Alex's surprise, he then took her hand and squeezed it.

"When we find him," he said, "I'm going to kill him."

They were just starting to figure out a new strategy as Alex updated the group text and her social media when her phone rang.

"What's up?" she said.

"I found him," said Luke.

Alex's eyes widened. Aaron, who could hear the call, nearly yelled, "Where?"

"At the ferry station."

Alex drove to the station as fast as she could. She knew Luke had already scoured the place. Had Logan been hiding somewhere?

When they arrived, Aaron barely let her stop the car before he ran inside. By the time she'd parked, she came inside to see Aaron hugging Logan, Logan sobbing in his uncle's arms.

There were also a number of police officers who were speaking with Aaron.

"What happened?" she asked Luke.

"Apparently, he sneaked onboard the last ferry but was caught before it left." Luke raised an eyebrow. "How old is this kid, again?"

"Eleven going on thirty." Alex laughed. "Aaron is never going to let that kid out of his sight."

"Based on how scared he looked, I don't think Logan will want to go anywhere any time soon."

When Aaron and Logan were finally allowed to leave, Alex offered to give them a ride to Aaron's car. But Aaron declined, telling her it wasn't far.

He barely looked at her as he spoke, and she knew that their ceasefire was probably over.

Luke came up to her after Logan and Aaron had left. "You okay?" he asked.

Alex felt the tears welling up again. "No," she whimpered. "I'm not okay."

CHAPTER TWENTY-TWO

Christmas was a strange affair in the Morrison household. Logan had barely spoken about his running away, while Pen had been tearful on and off leading up to the holiday. During the morning when they opened presents, Logan seemed sullen and uninterested in any of his gifts. Pen, at least, seemed more excited than her brother.

Aaron was just tired. So tired that it didn't seem to matter how many hours of sleep he got. Not only was he worried about the kids, he missed Alex.

Every night, he thought of how she'd shown up to help him, no questions asked. It only made him think that her angry words had been lies. Which begged the question: what should he believe? That she cared, or that she didn't? He couldn't figure out the enigma that was Alexandra Gray.

During Christmas afternoon, Aaron went to Logan's room, knowing that he needed to have this conversation while also dreading it.

Logan was lying on his bed and staring at the ceiling.

The fact that he wasn't even playing a video game made Aaron even more anxious.

"Can we talk?" said Aaron. He sat down on the bed next to Logan.

Logan shrugged. "Whatever."

"I think you need to tell me what happened that night. Why did you run away?"

Logan's mouth twisted into a scowl. "You'll just get mad if I tell you."

Aaron forced himself to take a deep breath. "I won't get mad. I promise. I just want the truth."

Logan didn't look convinced, but he eventually said, "I was tired of living here. I wanted to go back to Seattle. To my old school. My old friends. I don't have any friends here. This place is boring. It's stupid. It's a bunch of old ladies in golf carts and no kids."

"I know it's a big change from the city. But we needed a fresh start. You guys weren't happy in Seattle, either."

Logan sat up. "Yeah, we were! We were happy there. Then you come in and take us here, and you act like you're my dad, but you're not. You're not him. You'll never be him."

"I'm not trying to replace him. But he's gone, Logan. I'm trying the best I can for you guys."

"No, you're not. You're never here. You didn't even know I was gone until later."

Aaron felt like he was in an alternate reality. "Not home? Logan, I'm probably more home even than you or Pen."

"You're just in your office." Logan wrapped his arms around his knees. "That doesn't count."

Aaron felt ashamed that Logan was right. In his attempt to give the kids space, he'd inadvertently kept them at arm's length.

"I'm sorry that I haven't been around enough. It wasn't because of you or your sister. I didn't want to impose because you're right: I'm not your dad. I can never replace him or your mom," said Aaron.

"Whatever," said Logan, his standard reply.

"Not 'whatever.' I want us to be a family." Aaron touched Logan's arm. "Look at me. I love you. You know that, right?"

Logan just nodded tightly.

"What did you think would happen after you'd run away? I'd just let you go? Where were you going to stay? Did you have any plan at all?" asked Aaron, although he already knew the answers to those questions.

"I thought I could get to Seattle and stay with Malcolm. He kept telling me I should come back." Malcolm was one of Logan's friends, although Aaron had never met him or his family.

"Did he put you up to this?"

"No! It's not his fault. It was my idea."

Aaron was slowly putting the pieces together. He'd been so wrapped up in Alex that he hadn't been a good parent lately. And now, he realized that Logan's bad behavior had more than likely just been attempts to gain his attention.

"Is that why you keep getting in trouble in school?" asked Aaron. "So you'll get my attention?"

Logan shrugged. "Maybe."

"I'll do better. How about we try to do something fun,

just us, once a month? And I'll do the same thing with Pen. We'll do more family outings, too."

"Every time we go out, you just get mad at me."

Aaron sighed because Logan wasn't wrong. Aaron had become so focused on his nephew's bad behavior that he hadn't considered why he was acting out. "I won't get mad. I can do better. Let me prove it to you."

Aaron's heart squeezed as he saw the glimmers of hope in Logan's face.

"I was so scared when I found out you'd run away, you know," said Aaron.

Logan looked surprised. "Really? Why?"

"Why? You could've gotten hurt. Someone could've kidnapped you. You tried to sneak onto the ferry, and what if you'd gotten stuck and no one could find you—"

"You're getting mad again."

Aaron took a breath. Then another. "I'm not mad at you. I'm madder at myself. But you have to promise me that you won't do that again. If you want my attention, tell me. I'll always make time for you."

"Okay."

Aaron hugged the boy and was overjoyed when Logan hugged him back. But when he gave Logan a smacking kiss, Logan groaned and pushed him away.

"Boys aren't supposed to kiss!" Logan wiped the kiss from his cheek, scowling.

"Oh, how wrong you are about that."

As Aaron went to his office, he couldn't help but feel even guiltier. Clearly, this Alex obsession of his was unhealthy. He'd become so fixated on her that he hadn't seen what was going on right under his nose.

When she'd told him that they weren't good for each other, well, she was right. He needed to focus on his kids. Not on dating, and definitely not on finding a replacement mother.

Was that just an excuse because you're lonely? he asked himself.

Aaron didn't want to consider the actual answer to that question. As he sat down heavily in his office chair, he knew what he needed to do, and he wasn't looking forward to it in the least.

THE DAY after Christmas was a slow time for the bookstore. Alex normally found it frustrating, if not downright boring, but this time she was relieved.

She didn't need one more person to look at her concernedly and ask her how she was holding up. Or worse, asking her what went wrong.

I heard about the signing. Do you think she thought the island wasn't worth her time? one man asked Alex that morning.

Are you sure you had the right date? Maybe she meant next year instead. That remark nearly made Alex deck the woman, like she had no idea how to read when she owned a damn bookstore.

Chris finally came in for his shift, allowing Alex to retreat to her office. But as she went over her spreadsheets, she only felt more hopeless. She'd been issuing refunds since the signing, and with every one that was processed, the little nest egg she'd gained from all of the preorders dwindled to practically nothing.

She knew that she was going to have to close. The

thought didn't scare her now. It only made her feel sad and resigned.

There was a knock on her door that startled her from her thoughts. Then before she could even respond, Aaron was walking inside and shutting the door behind him.

"We need to talk," he said.

Alex frowned. "Um, I'm at work right now."

"Are you busy?"

Alex had to admit that she wasn't. Scowling, she gestured for Aaron to sit.

She couldn't help but notice that he looked thinner, the circles beneath his eyes darker. She had the urge to take him home, feed him a nice meal, and tuck him into bed.

"You look terrible," she said.

He laughed gruffly. "Wow, thanks. I can always count on you to be honest, at least."

"Sorry. But you look tired. How's Logan? How are you?"

He sighed. "We're bumping along. Logan and I talked." Aaron stared down at his hands, like he was preparing himself for what he had to say next. "Our conversation that day, before Logan ran away..."

Alex's cheeks flamed with embarrassment. "I said some stupid things. I was tipsy. I always run my mouth when I'm like that. I'm sorry."

"No, I'm sorry. I said some stupid things, too." Aaron sifted his fingers through his hair. "But I thought about what you said. And after the Logan ordeal, I realized that you were right."

"About what?" Alex let out an unsteady laugh. "I can't even remember everything I said."

"You said that we weren't good for each other. That we weren't meant to be anything but a fling." His gaze met hers. "I didn't want to believe you, but I realized that you were right. I was so intent on getting you to see my way of thinking that I didn't see how I was ignoring my own kids. To the point that Logan felt like he had to run away to get my attention."

Alex's chest constricted. "You're being too hard on yourself."

"Am I? I promised at my brother's funeral that I'd take care of his kids, but I've been selfish. I was lonely, and I was too focused on our relationship. Whatever it is." He shook his head.

"So what now?" Alex whispered.

"That's the thing. There is no 'what now.'" His gaze was steely now, his jaw set. "We can't keep seeing each other. It's not good for either of us. Tell me, have you been happy? Because it seems like we only make each other miserable."

Alex couldn't come up with a reply, because she knew that he was right. She'd never been able to date men that were good for her. Why should she trust herself now? Aaron obviously knew what he was talking about.

Even as she told herself that, she felt shattered. Her mouth dry, she said, "So we're just going to avoid each other?"

"No. I mean, we don't need to do that. But I'm also considering returning to Seattle in the spring, once the school year is over."

"What? You don't have to leave."

Aaron looked away from her. "I think it's best. I also

know that when it comes to you, my self-control is basically nonexistent."

"I guess I'll take that as a compliment." Alex tried to speak lightly, but her voice was hoarse.

When Aaron got up and held out his arms for a hug, Alex wanted to decline. But she also wanted to touch him one last time.

He hugged her closely, and she buried her face in his shoulder. She inhaled his scent, memories of their last time together in bed flooding her mind.

When she tipped her head back to look at him, he caressed her jaw. His fingers danced across her face with a gentleness that made her want to cry.

"Alex." He nearly growled her name. "God, Alex."

Then he kissed her. The kiss seared straight through Alex's soul, until she didn't know where she began, and he ended. She wondered how she could ever have thought she could let this man go.

He kissed her like a man starved. He kissed her like he knew he'd never kiss her again.

He broke the kiss and pushed her away, groaning. When she tried to touch him, he said sharply, "No. No. This is over."

Aaron sounded like he was trying to convince himself more than he was trying to convince her.

"I can't keep doing this." Aaron looked at her like she was both heaven and hell in one human body. "You can't keep doing this to me."

She wanted to shake him. She wanted to keep kissing him. But she also had too much pride to beg.

He left, muttering a goodbye. Alex returned to her desk, put her head down, and cried.

CHAPTER TWENTY-THREE

Alex sat in the living room as Felicity retrieved some of her clothes from her bedroom. Felicity hadn't seemed inclined to talk yet, and Alex wasn't sure if she ever would.

Alex was about to turn on the TV when Felicity emerged. After putting the clothes in a bag, Felicity said quietly, "We should talk."

Felicity settled on the chair next to Alex. It had always been her favorite chair, and Alex hadn't sat in it since Felicity had left.

"I'm sorry," said Alex. She felt like she was going to burst. "I should never have gone behind your back like that. It was a shitty thing to do."

Felicity tucked a piece of blond hair behind her ear. "Can you tell me something?"

"Anything."

"Did you ever think that Aaron liked me? Or were you just putting us together because it helped you?"

Shame cut through Alex like a knife. "I can't speak for

Aaron, but I'm pretty sure he was interested. I don't think he would've kept going on dates with you if he hadn't been."

"Or that you persuaded him to do so because you thought it'd make me happy."

Alex wanted to disappear under the nearest rock. Groaning, she replied, "I don't even know anymore. I'm so mixed up."

"You know, I wasn't so much hurt that you made a bargain with Aaron. If I'd been in your shoes, I might've done the same thing." Felicity tucked in her chin, her gaze on her feet. "But the fact that Aaron wasn't even interested in me... You can't know how humiliating that is."

"Liss. He was. He asked you out before I ever became involved."

Now Felicity's gaze met Alex's. "But he hadn't stopped thinking about you. Don't try to tell me that wasn't true."

"I don't know," Alex hedged. "You'd have to ask him."

Felicity groaned. "God, this is all so stupid. This is like the worst kind of high school drama." She laughed and groaned a second time.

"I do want you to come back to our apartment. I've missed you. It's been lonely, being here without you." Alex swallowed against the lump in her throat. "And as far as Aaron goes, we ended things. He said he's leaving the island once the school year is over."

Felicity sat up straight. "Seriously? He just moved here."

"I guess it just wasn't working for them."

"There's something you're not telling me."

Alex spread her fingers, palms up. "We slept together.

We had a fling. I told him that was all it could be. He finally agreed. The end."

Felicity narrowed her eyes. "Why do you sound like you're about to start crying?"

"I'm always crying. I cried at a dog food commercial last night."

"You know what I mean." Felicity got up to sit next to Alex. "You love him, don't you?"

Alex wanted to die. She wanted to run out the door and never come back. Defeated, she just replied, "It doesn't matter. I fucked it up."

"Look, I'm mad at you, although seeing you like this makes me feel a little better."

Alex snorted. "Wow, thanks."

"But it sounds like you and Aaron have something real."

"Liss, he went on dates with you because he's convinced I wouldn't make a good stepmom. He doesn't think I'm worth the commitment." Now Alex was starting to cry.

"He doesn't think that, or *you* think that?"

"Is there a difference?"

"Look, if you love him, and if you think he has feelings for you, you should tell him. You guys have a lot of baggage, so it makes sense that things got messy." Felicity took Alex's hand and squeezed it. "I can tell that you really care about this guy."

Alex started crying. "Oh God. I do. I love him. I never meant to fall for him. It just happened. I never wanted it to happen, I swear to you—"

Felicity shushed her. Alex let herself be comforted, but she soon forced herself to stop crying.

"Here you are, consoling me, when I should be consoling you," sniffled Alex. "I never wanted to humiliate you, you know."

"I know. Your intentions weren't malicious. They usually aren't." Felicity smiled sadly. "But you and I know that sometimes you can't cross the street before looking."

"It keeps things exciting."

Felicity looked down at her hands. "I heard about the signing. I'm sorry."

"Oh lord, I can't talk about that. I can't think about the bookstore right now. Everything is just a hot mess, isn't it? My life is a dumpster fire."

"Do you think you'll have to close the store?"

Alex sighed. "I've already started on that path. The store can't survive. Not with Aaron increasing the rent."

Felicity's eyes widened. "He's still doing that? After everything?"

"He hasn't told me otherwise. Why would he change his mind? It's his building. He can charge what he wants."

Felicity pinched Alex's arm, hard enough to make Alex yelp.

"What was that for?" she yelled.

"Look, you can feel sorry for yourself if you want, but the Alex I know is a fighter. She's innovative. She doesn't just give up. So the signing was a bust? What else can you do? Can you raise funds elsewhere? What about a business loan? Have you asked Luke? He has money."

Alex felt a little dizzy. "I'm not asking my brother-in-law for money."

"Then your sister."

"You think Jocelyn is going to lend me money?" Alex laughed. "You're insane."

"You never know. You won't know unless you ask."

"She'd just tell me to let the place go. She's never agreed with me buying it in the first place."

"Or she's just been worried that you'll get your heart broken."

Alex shook her head. "Whose side are you on?"

"Yours, mine. Ours." Felicity's eyes were shining now. "You're one of my best friends. Even when you drive me crazy, I still love you."

Alex's throat closed. "You're going to make me start crying again."

"Then instead, let's start planning. And maybe I'll help you write the perfect speech to persuade Jocelyn that she should totally lend you the money."

THE NEW YEAR came and went, blessedly uneventful. Logan seemed calmer, and Aaron hoped that his ordeal had taught him a thing or two about acting out.

Pen, though, was distant. Aaron tried to engage his niece, asking her about what books she was reading, but she'd give one-word answers and not much else. She generally stayed in her room, which didn't change when the kids returned to school after winter break.

Aaron wondered if he needed to worry about Pen acting out now. He had a difficult time imagining the mature thirteen-year-old running away or getting into any kind of trouble. He almost wished she would. At least then he could maybe begin to figure out what was going on.

One weekend, Aaron impulsively decided to take all of them to Seattle. Not just for something to do, but also to visit their parents' graves. They hadn't been back since they'd moved to Hazel Island in the fall.

After spending most of the morning and afternoon wandering downtown Seattle, including buying both kids new clothes and shoes, they made their way to the cemetery.

They were both silent on the ride there. He'd never seen them this quiet, not since the funeral.

Pen had the flowers they'd picked out cradled in her arms. As Aaron looked at her out of the corner of his eye, he could imagine the amazing woman she'd grow up to be one day.

It was cold and misty, but it seemed suitable for the occasion. The cemetery was mostly deserted.

When they arrived at the two gravestones, Aaron was surprised that they were both so clean and shiny still. He would've thought the weather in the past year would've made its mark.

"Should we say something?" asked Logan, looking up at Aaron.

"You can if you want."

Pen kneeled down and placed the white roses—Ashley's favorite—on the graves. She then traced the letters of her parents' names.

Aaron's throat closed. Grief threatened to make him fall apart, but he forced back the sobs. He needed to stay strong for the two kids who needed him for support.

"Mom, I read one hundred books last year," said Pen proudly. "You always said you wanted to read that many, but I don't know if you ever did. Well, I did, and I'm going to try to read even more this year."

"I got an A on my math test," said Logan. "I would've gotten an A+, except my teacher took off points because she said my handwriting was bad."

"It *is* bad." Pen stood, wiping her hands on her pants. "I could barely read the note you left."

"Pen," said Aaron, warningly.

"She's just jealous that she never gets As on her math tests," was Logan's reply.

Before they descended into another sibling squabble, Aaron asked them to say a few more things to their parents. Logan talked about his adventure, as he called it, making sure to emphasize that he was basically arrested when he was caught trying to sneak onto the ferry.

Pen just rolled her eyes at this. She then told her parents that she was going to try out for the school play next week and hoped she'd get more than just a part in the chorus.

Aaron's eyes widened in surprise at that declaration. He hadn't heard a peep from her about a play.

"It's cold," complained Logan. "Can we go?"

Pen was shivering, too. Aaron handed her the keys and told her he'd be there in a few minutes.

After the kids left, Aaron stood and gazed down at the graves in silence. Seeing Jason and Ashley's names and being reminded of how young they were made Aaron want to scream in agony.

Mostly, though, he just missed them. Their absence was a hole in his heart that could never be filled again.

"I don't know why you had to die," said Aaron quietly. His breath puffed white in the cold air. "Not when you had two amazing children to take care of. But I promised that I'd take care of them."

He sighed. "Although I haven't done the greatest job lately. Logan, you know, he's been a challenge. I was terrified when he ran away. I thought for sure that I'd messed up for good. I know if something had happened to him..."

Aaron couldn't bear to think about that possibility.

Later, he wouldn't know if he'd heard an actual voice, or if he'd simply imagined it. In that moment, he heard a voice that sounded eerily like Jason's say, *You're doing your best. Stop beating yourself up already.*

Aaron blinked. He turned, looking for the source of the sound, but there was no one there. He was the only person in the cemetery.

The hairs on the back of Aaron's neck stood on end. It didn't help that the mist and soft rain made the place even spookier.

But as he returned to the car, the kids on their phones, Aaron felt a sense of peace he hadn't felt in a long time.

"Hey," he said to the rearview mirror, "are you guys happy?"

Logan glanced up. "Huh?"

"I mean, happy that you came to live with me?"

Pen caught his gaze in the mirror. "Uncle Aaron, that's a dumb question. You're the only one we wanted to come live with."

Logan just nodded vigorously and then returned to his video game.

Aaron knew he would never replace their parents. But

as they returned home and the sun peeked through the clouds, Aaron wondered if it was Jason again telling him to keep going.

He stared out at the horizon, toward Hazel Island, for the entire trip back. Not just longing for the island itself, but for the woman living there who'd captured his heart one moonlit night and had never let it go.

CHAPTER TWENTY-FOUR

"You want me to buy you out," repeated Luke.

Aaron, trying to keep his impatience in check, gritted out, "Yes."

Luke glanced down at the amount that Aaron had proposed for the buy-out of the building in question. "Did you forget a zero here?"

"No. That's the right amount."

Luke steepled his fingers, assessing Aaron. They were currently sitting in Luke's office, which was pretty much what Aaron would've expected Luke Wright's office to look like. Lots of dark brown leather furniture, similarly dark rugs, and staid artwork on the walls. The only surprise was that Luke didn't have any antlers or deer heads affixed to the walls or a cigar smoking in an ashtray on his desk.

"You realize this would make me my sister-in-law's landlord," said Luke. "I'm not sure even I want to take that task on."

"I realize it could be a conflict of interest, but you're one of the few people—only people—on the island who I'd trust to take this on."

Luke smiled. "That's nice of you. Naive, but nice." His smile disappeared quickly. "Tell me really why you're doing this. Because if there's something wrong with the building, and you're trying to cheat me—"

"You'd have it inspected. As far as I know, the only thing that needs updating soon is the roof. The plumbing has seen better days."

Luke looked down at the document again. Aaron waited on tenterhooks, feeling like he was going to explode from anticipation.

Selling the building at this low of a price would be an absolute steal for Luke and a huge loss for Aaron. He'd worked day and night to figure out if he could afford it.

"I don't get why you're selling it this low. You haven't told me the real reason yet," said Luke. Based on his expression, he wasn't going to let Aaron get away without spilling his guts.

Aaron sighed. "I'm in love with your sister-in-law," he confessed finally. "I can't be her landlord. Not if she's going to see that I care more about her than I do about a stupid building."

"Practically speaking, this is an idiotic decision," Luke pointed out sagely. "Together, you both could handle the tenants and give Alex's store a discount in rent as well."

Aaron's expression was mulish. "I agree. It *is* a stupid thing to do. That's why it's necessary. This isn't about money. It's about showing Alex how much I love her and want to make a life with her."

Luke said nothing for a long moment. He eventually rose from his chair and got himself a glass of what looked like whiskey. He offered Aaron one, but Aaron declined. The last thing he needed right now was to muddle his brain with liquor.

"You know, two years ago, I would've told you to get the hell out of my office," said Luke, swirling the whiskey around. "I would've thought you were out to swindle me. Inspections can miss things. Or you'd recommend some guy who'd neglect to mention that the building's foundation was sinking. You know, something like that."

"I had no idea you were so cynical. Or paranoid," muttered Aaron.

Luke chuckled. "I'm not, generally speaking. But I also know that when it comes to money, you should be suspicious of people. That's just the world we live in."

He turned to face Aaron. "Did you know that I married my wife to get my inheritance? Based on your face, you didn't. It's not a well-known fact, but I wondered if Alex would've told you. At any rate, I thought I married her just for my gain. Hers, too. I soon realized there was more to it than that. She showed me that there are way more important things in life than money or inheritances."

Aaron was struggling not to tap his foot from sheer impatience. "Wright, deal or no deal?"

Luke laughed. "Sorry, apparently I'm in a philosophical mood today." He finished his glass and set it down with a thump. "You're in love with Alex?" he asked frankly.

Aaron, tired of looking up at Luke, stood up. He was rather pleased to note that he was at least an inch taller than the man.

"I already said as much," Aaron replied.

"And what happens when you sell this place for a penny? Are you in deep shit financially?"

"I can make it work."

"Because I'd rather not agree if it means Alex is going to watch you struggle. She has a soft heart, you know, despite what she acts like. She's a lot like Jocelyn in that way. But you also have no guarantee that I won't raise the rent just like you have."

Aaron scoffed. "And risk your wife's displeasure? I doubt it."

Luke chuckled. "Very astute of you." He then stuck out his hand. "Deal. I'll take the place off of your hands. But only if you promise that you'll never break Alex's heart. Because not only will you have to contend with me, you'll have to deal with Jocelyn. Let me tell you, she's terrifying when she wants to be."

"She already came after me a few months ago. She said pretty much the exact same thing."

Luke's eyes widened. "She did? Damn, she didn't say a word to me." He scowled. "So much for complete honesty in marriage."

Now Aaron was tapping his foot. "As much as I'm enjoying our meeting, I have more important things to attend to."

"Oh, of course. You have some groveling to do." Luke leaned closer. "Pro-tip: don't mention a single thing she did wrong. You won't get very far. Act like everything is your fault, even if you know she has a little bit to blame."

"Noted, thanks," said Aaron wryly.

WHEN ALEX LOOKED up at the sound of the entrance bell and saw Aaron, she had intense déjà vu. She couldn't help but remember that day in early fall when they'd first realized who the other person was.

This time, though, Aaron had an intent look on his stupidly handsome face. When he spotted Alex at the register, he stalked toward her like some kind of jungle cat.

"Welcome, let me know if you need help finding anything," she said pleasantly.

"Alex. I need to talk to you."

Alex was making notes to make it seem like she was busy. "I'm working."

Aaron glanced around the store. "There's no one here."

"There are two customers in the back corner reading. Besides, I have shelves to stock."

Despite her cool words, her heart was pounding like mad. Inhaling his scent, hearing his voice—both were nearly too much for her to handle.

She was also annoyed at how much she'd simply missed him. She missed texting him random things she found on the Internet. She missed hearing his voice when he just called to talk about nothing. She missed his arms holding her close after they'd made love.

"Alex," he repeated. "Look at me."

She did, but not without glaring at him, too. It was easier than letting herself burst into tears.

"I love you," he said.

Alex nearly snapped the pencil she held in two. "What?"

"I love you. I want to make a life with you."

Alex was shaking her head now; she walked away from Aaron without a reply.

"Did you hear me?" asked Aaron.

"I heard you. I'm just not going to respond."

Aaron caught her by the wrist, forcing her to face him again. "I want you, Alexandra Gray. You and no one else. I'm in love with you."

She swallowed. "Aaron, this thing between us... It keeps giving us whiplash. 'I want you, I don't want you.' It's exhausting. Aren't you tired? Because I am."

"I could never get tired of you. I wake up thinking about you; I go to sleep dreaming of you. I see you every-where." Aaron ran his fingers through his hair. "It's driving me *crazy*. I see a woman with your hair color and think it's you, and when it's not, it's so painful I can barely breathe."

Alex felt her lower lip start trembling. "Aaron, please—"

He got down on one knee. Alex's eyes widened. When he didn't pull out what she expected, and instead pulled out a piece of paper, she gaped at him.

"You came all the way here to give me..." She squinted at the document and then flushed with outrage. "A fucking *bill*? Jesus, you have gigantic balls, don't you?"

"No, shit, you don't understand—" Aaron ripped the invoice in two. "I sold the building. I'm not your landlord anymore. I took a huge loss and God knows when I'll dig myself out of that hole. But I did it because I love you more than I love money, or real estate, or my pride. I nearly begged your brother-in-law to buy the place."

Alex picked up the ripped pieces of paper, and then she started laughing. "Seriously?"

Aaron didn't look so amused. "Yeah, I'm serious. I'm on one knee, for God's sake!"

Alex just kept giggling. She laughed so hard she nearly collapsed to the floor. Finally, she helped Aaron stand up and then yanked his head down for a hard kiss.

Aaron's outrage softened within seconds. He wrapped his arms around her and kissed her until they were both panting for air.

"You love me?" she asked, smiling like an idiot.

"I'll keep saying it until you believe me."

"I believe you. And I love you, too. I didn't want to. You piss me off. You're bossy as shit. You come in here and basically demand to see me—"

Aaron shut her up with a kiss. Alex didn't have the heart to tell him he couldn't keep doing that to keep her quiet.

The kiss only ended when someone cleared their throat. Chris, bless his heart, was looking at anything but at the red-faced couple.

"Uh, Alex, I hate to interrupt this very touching Hallmark-movie moment, but I can't find the newest shipment of books from Harper Collins," he said.

Alex could barely stifle the laughter still bubbling in her throat. She patted Aaron on the chest and said in a prim voice, "Yes, I think those terms are agreeable. I'll send you a confirmation email later today."

Aaron's lips twitched. "Sounds good, ma'am." Then he gave her one last loud kiss, whispered that he'd see her tonight, and left.

Alex's cheeks were red hot, and they only got hotter when she saw Chris' smirk.

"Glad you two lovebirds worked it out," he said. "I was tired of watching you mope around the store."

"I'm still your boss. Get back to work."

"I'm trying. But there are these weirdos making a scene in the middle of the store. Could you tell them to quit it?"

Alex stuck out her tongue, but then she started laughing again, so joyous her heart felt like it would burst.

EPILOGUE

When Logan walked across the stage for his middle school graduation, Aaron was surprised to find that he was holding back tears. Alex reached over and squeezed his hand, which just made him want to cry even more.

Apparently having kids meant crying at the drop of a hat. Or maybe, Aaron mused, it was just pure relief that they got to this day at all.

Logan waved at the crowd before taking his diploma. Then, because he never failed to be the attention seeker he was, he attempted a cartwheel on stage but nearly collided with the principal instead.

Aaron grimaced. "Christ almighty," he said, getting up. "Can we not end up in the hospital today of all days?"

Logan scampered off stage, unharmed. Principal Foster adjusted his glasses and shook his head.

"I'm sure he's happy Logan is graduating," said Alex quietly, laughing under her breath.

"You mean no longer his problem? Yeah, I'm sure he's thrilled," replied Aaron.

"I'd never do that," scoffed Pen. "He's such a weirdo."

Aaron couldn't disagree. Logan would never be an easy child. They'd had their share of battles over the past year. When Aaron had decided to stay on Hazel Island to be close to Alex, the kids hadn't been thrilled at first. They'd been looking forward to returning to Seattle and their old schools and friends.

But Alex's presence, along with Aaron's renewed sense of purpose, had helped weather any storms. Sending the kids to therapy sessions had also helped. Aaron had been amazed when Logan had returned home one day, talking about his emotions and how he could respond to them constructively. It had been as if the child Logan had suddenly morphed into a young man.

The rest of the graduation ceremony continued without further mishap. When Logan found them afterward, Aaron didn't have the heart to scold him. He looked so proud of himself, an expression Aaron hadn't seen on his nephew's face before.

"Congratulations," said Aaron, hugging Logan for the brief moment Logan allowed him. "We're very proud of you."

Logan wiggled out of Aaron's embrace and frowned. "Don't hug me in front of everybody!" he hissed. He glanced around, but his peers were too busy with their own families to notice the hug.

To Aaron's annoyance, Logan seemed perfectly happy to accept Alex's hug. The smarmy little brat even grinned at

Aaron. *This one is growing up way too fast*, Aaron thought to himself in despair.

Pen, being fourteen, muttered *congrats* under her breath and returned to scrolling on her phone. Aaron couldn't really blame her. The last time she'd tried to hug her brother, he'd farted loudly and had run off laughing like a maniac.

The family went to lunch at Lyn's Eatery afterward. It was a lovely day in mid-June, the sun bright while the sea breeze kept the day from getting too warm.

Despite the breeze, Aaron struggled to keep from sweating. In his pocket sat the ring he'd purchased weeks ago, waiting for the right moment to propose to Alex.

Alex, wearing oversized sunglasses, smiled at him and said, "What? You keep staring at me."

"Because you're so beautiful," said Aaron.

Logan made a gagging noise. Aaron kicked him under the table.

Maybe I shouldn't have done this with the kids around, thought Aaron as they ate their lunches. Despite Logan's behavior, both kids had bonded with Alex. During the times when she was too busy with the bookstore to come over for dinner, both kids would be visibly disappointed.

Aaron had been extra grateful for Alex when Pen had started her period around the holidays. Although he was happy to buy whatever products his niece needed, Pen had found his concern so embarrassing that she'd relied solely on Alex for help and advice.

"I've bought tampons and pads before," Aaron had groused to Alex one night.

Alex's lips had quirked up. "Really? I'm impressed."

"I mean, my girlfriend at the time had to message me a picture of what she needed. But I managed. It's not a big deal."

Alex had patted his shoulder. "You're a good uncle and boyfriend. Next time, I'll have you get tampons for me, how about that?"

Aaron barely tasted his lunch. Alex kept giving him strange looks. Considering that he'd barely spoken throughout lunch, he couldn't blame her.

He was considering if he should wait to ask her in private when she said point-blank, "Are you okay? You look like you're going to be sick."

Logan's face lit up. "Are you going to puke?"

"You're disgusting." Pen's nose wrinkled.

With all three sets of eyes on him, Aaron suddenly felt extra hot under his collar. Christ, was it a hundred degrees out here? He needed a cold drink. Or five.

"I'm fine," he said through gritted teeth.

Alex touched his forehead with the back of her hand. "Hmm. You're a little warm."

"I bet it's dysentery. Or Ebola. Did you know you bleed out of your eyeballs when you have Ebola? I saw a video about it. It was so gross." Logan nearly rubbed his hands with glee.

"Logan! I'm eating!" whined Pen.

As the kids bickered, Aaron rubbed his temples.

"Are you sure you're okay?" whispered Alex.

"I'm fine. Seriously. And it's not Ebola."

Aaron decided he'd better wait until the kids were elsewhere to propose. But his new plan was dashed when his jacket, which he'd draped over the back of the chair and which held the ring, fell to the ground. Pen reached down to pick up the little velvet box that had landed near her foot.

Before Aaron could snatch the box away, Pen opened it. Her eyes widened. "Oh my God."

Aaron took the box and snapped it closed. Alex had a confused expression on her face.

"Aaron...?" asked Alex, staring at the box in his hand. "Is that...?"

"What? What is it?" Logan demanded. "What happened?"

When no one answered Logan, he said more loudly, "WHAT IS HAPPENING?" while Pen kept saying over and over, "Oh my God, oh my God!"

Aaron sighed. Then, standing up, he yelled at his niece and nephew, "You two! Be quiet. Now."

Considering Aaron rarely raised his voice, it was so surprising that both kids snapped their mouths shut.

Then, going down on one knee, Aaron reopened the box to a shocked Alex. "I meant to do this so much better," he admitted. He could feel the stares of everyone around them, and it made him start to sweat again. "But Alex, will you make me the happiest man on this earth and marry me?"

Alex's eyes were shining with tears—tears of laughter. "Oh my God." She covered her mouth with her hand, giggling. Then, composing herself, she said, "Of course I'll marry you, you idiot."

Both Pen and Logan erupted into cheers. Their audience of fellow restaurant-goers applauded. And Aaron placed the ring on his new fiancée's finger and kissed her, no longer caring one iota what anyone else thought.

FELICITY LINDEN HAD NEVER BEEN fond of living by herself. The ironic thing was that for most of her adulthood, she'd done just that. When Alex had told her that she was moving in with Aaron, Felicity hadn't been surprised. But it would mean that, once again, Felicity would be on her own.

Felicity didn't mind her own company. It was more when it was dark, and she was lying in bed unable to sleep, that the creaks and groans and whistling winds made her paranoid. She tended to check the locks on her windows and doors twice, thrice, sometimes four times.

In her latest apartment—she couldn't afford the one she'd lived in with Alex on her own—she wished she hadn't caved to getting one on the first floor. It was too close to *people.*

With the birthmark that stained the left side of her face, Felicity had never been fond of people in general. The fact that she had more than one friend tended to astonish her whenever she remembered that fact.

Settling in for the evening at her laptop, Felicity chewed on her lower lip as she began writing a scene. No one in her life knew that she didn't write resumes much anymore, but instead romance novels. She'd written ten already. The one drawback to having a roommate—and a nosey one at that —was the constant fear that Felicity's secret would come out.

In this scene, Felicity was struggling to convey that her lumberjack hero was, in fact, a softhearted cinnamon roll despite the rippling muscles and long beard.

Maybe he was too gruff in the opener, she thought to herself, making notes on a pad of paper. *Or I need to add more bits of niceness earlier on.*

She sighed. Some books didn't take much effort to write, but this one? It was like pulling teeth. Any time that happened, Felicity always worried the book wouldn't be well received.

As if reading her mind, her agent texted her for updates. Felicity glanced at her phone and grimaced. *Getting that chapter done???* it read, with the addition of lots of writing emojis, in case Felicity hadn't already gotten the message.

Amy was anything if not a great cheerleader. Sometimes Felicity wished her agent weren't quite so cheerful. It was like having a golden retriever constantly asking for attention.

Felicity forced herself to keep writing. But as she wrote one paragraph, then another, then deleted both, she ended up writing a total of twenty words. *So much for being productive tonight,* she groused.

She went to bed a few hours later, but not before she read a few more chapters of a steamy historical romance. When Felicity got to the first sex scene, she found herself blushing. It took a lot to make her blush these days. She'd written so many sex scenes that she was sure she was immune to them by now.

Apparently, though, she wasn't. As the scene heated up, so did Felicity's body. And brain.

Grabbing her laptop, she opened it and started typing. The words flowed from her fingers, almost as if someone else were doing it for her. By the time she was finished with that damn scene, she was grinning from ear to ear.

In the early hours of the morning, she dreamed. In the

dream was the lumberjack—Harley—wearing red plaid and carrying his ax. He was all muscles and calluses, his voice gruff yet velvety at the same time.

Harley was sweating, and his biceps bulged as he wiped his brow. Felicity watched him stack wood, but it didn't take long for him to notice her watching him.

Then—because dreams were strange things—she found herself on the ground under Harley, completely naked. He was kissing her body from head to toe. Felicity arched under him as he whispered dirty words into her ear.

When he parted her folds, playing with her, Felicity moaned. He sucked on the lobe of her ear as he gently stroked her clit.

As the orgasm built, Felicity heard a siren. And then right before she came, she woke up to the sound of a fire truck speeding past her apartment. It took her a moment to realize where she was. Groaning, she turned into her pillow, put her hand down her pajama pants, and finished herself off in just a few strokes.

She couldn't return to sleep at that point. Getting up, she padded to the kitchen to start making coffee. Only a few minutes later, someone knocked on her apartment door.

Frowning, Felicity waited for the person to leave. But the knocking just continued, more loudly this time. Sighing, she went to her door, prepared to tell the person off for bothering her this early in the morning.

But words fled when she opened the door to Harley. He was tall, bearded, and looked like he'd come straight from the woods.

"Harley," she whispered.

Harley—*no, not Harley*—gave her a strange look. "Um,

ma'am. I'm the gardener. I need to trim the bushes in front of your windows. I just wanted to let you know I'll be using a chainsaw so there'll be some noise."

Felicity nearly choked. "That's fine," she replied in a squeaky voice.

Then she slammed the door in Not-Harley's confused face and sunk to the floor, laughing hysterically.

A coffee addict and cat lover, USA Today bestselling author Iris Morland writes sparkling, swoon-worthy romances, including the Flower Shop Sisters and the Love Everlasting series.

If she's not reading or writing, she enjoys binging on Netflix shows and cooking something delicious.

She currently lives in Seattle with her partner, two cats, and an excessive number of houseplants.